Murder

Most Christian

Nicholas E Watkins

Murder Most Christian

The Eastbourne Murders Series

A Mandy Pile Mystery

About the Author

Nicholas Watkins lives on the South Coast and is the Author of the Tim Burr series of spy novels. He has four children. He worked as an accountant for many years in the City of London.

Murder Most Christian

Copyright © Nicholas E Watkins 2019

The right of Nicholas E Watkins to be identified as the Author of the Work has been asserted by him in accordance with the Copyright, Designs and patent Act 1988.

All rights reserved. No part of this publication my be reproduced, stored in a retrieval system, or transmitted, in any form or by any means without the prior written permission of the publisher, nor may be otherwise circulated in any form of binding or cover other than that in which it is published and without a similar condition being imposed on the subsequent purchaser.

All characters in this publication are fictional and any resemblance to real persons living or dead is purely coincidental.

Chapter 1

"Good night Mr Stein," she called as she closed the front door behind her. She decided to walk down the stairs rather than wait for the lift. Vera Reynolds had worked for her employer for over thirty years. She had been his personal assistant at Stein and Marsh Hedge Fund Managers. Now she called in most days to check in on her former boss.

The Bentley was waiting for her as she stepped onto to the Chelsea Embankment. Tim, the driver, had been with Stein nearly as long as she had. He and his wife lived in a mews cottage ten minutes from where his employer lived, in the mansion block over-looking the Thames in central London. The cottage where Tim lived had a garage where the Bentley was kept. Mr Stein was rich, very rich, and rich enough to buy a mews cottage for his chauffeur just so his car was close by.

Mrs Reynolds was also rich and lived nearby in Kensington with her husband. She had been given shares in Stein and Marsh and when it was sold, she had received a fortune. She could have easily taken a black cab or even walked, but it was her habit to call Tim to drive her back.

Like Raymond Stein, Vera and Tim lived slightly in the past. They had been together from the beginning, going through the struggles of the early years as they struggled to grow the business. But when Graham Marsh joined, the whole thing took off and soon it was a multi-billion pound company. Then, eight years ago, he had been killed in a car accident. Raymond had taken it badly and lost the drive to continue. He and Raymond had been like two peas in a pod. They would fuel each other's enthusiasm, planning and scheming for the next big deal. Vera always thought they were like two kids in a sweet shop.

With Graham's death Raymond had carried on, on his own for nearly a year, but it was clear he no longer derived the satisfaction he had from doing the next big deal. They were all rich and money was not the driving force any longer and without Graham's input, there seemed little point in continuing. Within eighteen months of his death the Company had been sold to an American Private Equity fund and they left.

Somehow they couldn't just let it go and separate. They were adrift and they continued their odd relationship. Tim had driven his boss to the office nearly everyday and waited for him, often late into the night to drive him home. He ran errands, shopping, dry cleaning and buying flowers. He did everything and anything Raymond asked. Sometimes, late at night, they would sit in the car and eat fish and chips.

Vera was also an integral part of Raymond's life. She organised haircuts, birthday cards, holidays and picked the cloth for his Saville Row suits. The three had formed part of the whole and when there was no longer a need, they couldn't help but continue.

"How was he today," asked Tim.

"Much the same, happy enough." She said. "Has he been out much lately?"

"He went to the theatre a few days back but it's rare for him to call me to drive him anywhere these days."

"He should try and enjoy himself more," she said.

"We all should, but it's hard as you get older to have the enthusiasm. The hustle bustle, adrenaline and excitement of those early days are hard to recreate. Everything now seems a bit mundane."

"The death of his wife, Joy hit him hard too. Has he shown any interest in that direction?"

Tim brought the car to a halt outside Vera's home. "I did run a young lady home a few times a while back. There was something going on but she was clearly the wrong sort."

"Gold digger?"

"More a prostitute, I'd say."

"Is she still on the scene?" said Vera.

"No, it just stopped."

"Probably for the best anyway," she waited while Tim got out and opened the door for her. Saying goodnight, she made her way in as the Bentley drove off into the night.

Raymond Stein had heard Vera leave and settled down in front of the television. These days he preferred to be alone. He had not planned it this way. He had planned to travel and do everything he had been too busy to do when he had been working. Joy, had it all worked out, the things they would do and the things they would see. It was not to be. Within a month of his selling Stein and Marsh she had been diagnosed with cancer. She was dead four months later.

He had withdrawn within himself and cut out the World. One night he had been persuaded to meet up with some old colleagues for dinner at the Savoy Hotel grill room on the strand. It had gone on later than he thought and after his friends left, he had gone into the American Bar for a nightcap while he waited for Tim to collect him. Tim had been in bed and needed to dress. Raymond could have easily ordered a taxi, but he knew Tim would have not liked that one little bit.

As he sat with his gin and tonic, he laughed inwardly at the situation. Tim was now a multi-millionaire but still liked to carry on working as his chauffeur. He, Vera and Tim liked it that way. It gave them purpose. It kept the bond alive between them.

Raymond suspected that they did it out of kindness. He had no family. His was an only child and his parents were both dead. His wife was dead and they never had children. His PA and driver were a sort of family and they knew, despite his great wealth, that he was lonely. Of course they could not keep the charade going forever but he appreciated their efforts.

"A penny for them," she said.

Raymond looked up at the stunning girl before him. He was surprised. The Savoy was very careful at screening young women that sat alone in the bar. The Savoy, like all the high end hotels were a draw to working girls, hoping to meet a wealthy, lonely businessman or celebrity. Usually they were spotted by security and discretely escorted off the premises.

For some reason, Raymond was drawn to her. Perhaps she reminded him of his wife but, for whatever the reason, he asked her to join him. It had grown from there. He knew he was being an old fool, but she brought a little life back into him. Even the mega rich can be lonely.

There was little of interest on the television. As he switched channels he wondered why she had suddenly disappeared from his life. He had been sure that there had been a genuine connection between them. She had been his companion for three or four months. He had even broached marriage. The last time he had seen her, Tim had driven her back to her flat, or at least to where she said she lived.

She just disappeared after that. He feared something had happened to her and had a private investigator look for her but to no avail. It was still a mystery. He reasoned that, even if she had only led him on for his money, she would be mad not to continue. They had a prenuptial agreement drawn up and he had altered his will to include her to the tune of fifty million pounds. Leaving, made no sense.

He was roused from his thoughts as the door bell rang. Grumbling he made his way to the hall. He spoke with the figure on the CCTV and opened the door.

"Well it's late?" he said as he turned and led the visitor towards the library.

His head was drawn back and before he could react, the knife was drawn across his throat. The hooded figure bent over him and stole the Rolex watch his wife had bought him.

Raymond Stein was still alive as the door to the street closed. Less than a minute later, life left him. His body would be found two days later by Vera.

Chapter 2

"Hurry up," John Draper called up the stairs to where Kelly Albright was getting ready in the bathroom.

She was looking in the mirror, applying her eye liner. It was a pleasant face, framed with thick dark hair and big appealing eyes. She was twenty nine years old, tall and slim. She put the finishing touches to her make-up and pouted her lips. She was pleased with the results. She had deliberately put on an overly short red dress that hugged her figure. It was a little bit of rebellion.

She hated Wednesday evenings, surrounded by the Alpha group at the Church. She had no interest in religion, no belief and certainly no desire to sit around for a couple of hours listening to the sanctimonious mumbo-jumbo at the local Church, but she had to go. John was a Christian and more to the point, his parents were Christians. A Church wedding mattered to them.

They wanted a Church wedding and they were paying. She had no family and the Drapers were setting the agenda for the big day. She had tried a number of churches in and around Eastbourne, but the last two Archbishops, of Canterbury were set on spreading the faith. To get married in Church, it was no longer good enough to turn up with your Christening certificate and have a chat with the Vicar. They wanted faith.

This demonstration of belief involved her and John turning up at the Church for six months on a Wednesday and joining the Alpha gang. The literature described the Alpha course as "an opportunity to explore the meaning of life" and a series of interactive sessions that freely explore the basics of the Christian faith. Kelly had no desire to explore the meaning of life, nor did she enjoy having an ear pounding every week, but she did love John and so put up with it.

Reluctantly she left the bathroom and made her way to John wjo was waiting in the car. She posed by the driver's side door and blew a kiss at him. "You are doing it on purpose," he commented. She wiggled her bottom, exaggerating the tightness of the dress and lent forward to his open window to give him an eyeful of her cleavage.

"We could just stay in and cuddle on the sofa," she smiled.

"Behave yourself," he laughed. "We have to go. Stop messing about and get in the car. You've made your point."

Feigning disappointment, she made her way to the passenger side and got in.

They had only been together for just over three months when he had proposed. She had been in Eastbourne a few weeks when she met John. There was nothing romantic about it. She had been working in a Kentucky Fried Chicken when he came in.

Something clicked between them and within weeks she had moved into his flat in the harbour development. The balcony overlooked the sea. Standing on that balcony beside her he had proposed. She remembered that the Moon had seemed enormous that night. She had taken it as a sign and said, "yes."

Sitting in the Church hall, watching a video of an ageing Irish rock star banging on about faith, she was seriously regretting her decision. What seemed a good idea, in a romantic moment on a moon lit night, was far from romantic when you were forced to listen to a bunch of happy clappies telling you how God had saved them from everything, from piles to drug addiction.

"Gather in a circle and let's contemplate in silence." Kelly had enough and rather than stand with her eyes shut for however long until they had completed their inner whatever, she left and went outside.

"For fucks sake," she said out loud as she rummaged in her handbag.

She had promised John she would give up smoking. She hadn't. It was just another sin to add to the list. She found her cigarettes and lit up. Inhaling, she felt better, or perhaps it was the satisfaction of this little act of rebellion. In any event, it was a relief to get away from the merry band inside the Church hall.

Looking for a place to go and a fresh start, she had settled on Eastbourne. She had been there before and had worked all along the South Coast, from Hastings to Brighton. "It will do," she had said as she walked along the sea front.

She felt it was fate. John walked into her life. Everything was well with the World. "Who knows," she thought. "Perhaps I will find faith as well."

She exhaled and laughed. "Not a chance," she said to herself.

She looked up. There was no moon tonight. She had made a point of moving away from the entrance into the shadows, out of sight of the group inside. The last thing she needed was the looks of condemnation from the congregation that would follow if they saw her nipping out for a quick fag.

The meditation ended and John settled into the group discussions. He expected Kelly to return soon. He had guessed that she had not entirely quit smoking and that was the reason for her absence. He glanced at the door and noted the brief look of disapproval from the Vicar. He refocused on the meeting.

He, unlike Kelly, was finding a meaning in the Alpha approach to the scriptures. His parents were firm believers and had taken him to Church every Sunday. He had attended Sunday school and had been confirmed. He believed.

Of course he had rebelled as all young do against their parents. University had been the catalyst for his rejection of his parent's beliefs. Now he was changing. He was actually finding his faith again. He was beginning to believe that it was more than fate that had brought Kelly and him together. Perhaps God was playing a hand in all things after all.

The man in his late sixties was telling the group how God had helped him. It was a tale of his son's drug addiction and how he had found strength to stand by him. He told how time and time again he had stepped in and taken him in and time and time again, his son had betrayed his trust and returned to addiction, also time and time again.

"It was God that allowed me to continue to sacrifice all in my bid to support him," the old man finished his testimony.

John looked at his watch. He couldn't understand why Kelly had not returned. It was over a half an hour since she had gone out, enough time to smoke a packet of cigarettes. He was annoyed. She realised how important a Church wedding was to his parents and she was jeopardising it.

Outside, he said goodnight to the gathering and looked around for her. She was nowhere to be seen. He guessed she must have gone home, taking a cab. He took out his cell phone and dialled her number. He heard it connect.

There was a scream from the far corner of the Church car park, shouting and the sound of people running to the source of the commotion. He instinctively ran into the darkness at the far corner of the car park.

A group had gathered by one of the cars. As he approached he was unclear what was happening. The group were silent, standing in silence as if frozen in time. The car door was open, creating the source of light, illuminating the scene around which they had gathered. He could not see what they were looking at.

As he came closer he did not hear the sound of a mobile phone ringing. He edged forward and saw her lying by the rear wheels of the parked car. The driver had opened the door to her car and then had seen Kelly. Her screams had drawn them.

John automatically disconnected the call from his phone. There was total silence as he came closer. Then the silence was broken by the sound of sobbing. He realised it was the sound of his own voice that was the source.

"Kelly, Kelly," he screamed as he knelt beside her.

He felt the stickiness on his hands as he cradled her head. Some one used their phone in torch mode, He realised he was kneeling in a large pool of blood, Kelly's blood. He had never seen so much blood in his life. John was nearly sick as he held her and sobbed.

She had been stabbed time and time again. The police sirens

could be heard in the distance. He trembled as he looked down on her. It was a sight he could never erase from his memory.

Chapter 3

Detective Sergeant Sam Shaw sat at his desk nursing a plastic cup of tepid tea. He reached over and took two paracetamol from their wrapping. He took a swig of tea, grimaced and swallowed the tablets. "I am getting too old for this shit," he mumbled to himself as he refocused on updating the computer log that filled the computer screen in front of him. Gradually one finger at a time, he entered the information.

The call had been logged at just before nine the previous evening and he had made his way to St Andrews Church, where a young woman was found murdered. It was now a full twelve hours later and he wanted to go home and get some sleep.

"No sign yet?" said Superintendent Taylor.

"Not a dicky."

"You will just have to hang on until you can hand over, sorry."

Sam responded with a grunt. He had been on the force over thirty years and the lack of resources was getting to him. Despite constant statements to the contrary by the Government, there was less money and it had to go further. Eastbourne Nick was now a Hub, not a Police Station, a Hub. The resources had been concentrated in the seaside town of Brighton, about twenty miles west along the coast.

"Bloody hub, we're not a hub, we are just an understaffed Police Station. There aren't enough coppers here to police a bowls match. It's a bloody joke."

"What was that?" asked Taylor.

"Nothing, I said I was looking forward to my bath tub and police bowls match." Taylor raised an eyebrow and walked off.

Sam settled back in his chair and waited. He must have dozed off. He realised that when he was being shaken by a constable that looked no more than twelve years old to him. "DS Shaw, DS Shaw," he was shaking his arm.

"What is it," said Sam, as he woke wondering what a copper was doing in his dream. It took him a few moments to understand that he had fallen asleep at his desk.

"The desk sergeant had been ringing your phone and you didn't answer. He sent me up to find you."

"Well you've found me. What is it?"

"Some one's turned up at the desk from Brighton Nick."

Sam collected his thoughts and with a groan got up from his seat and headed for the corridor and the steps leading to the ground floor. He pushed the door open and found himself behind the desk where the custody Sergeant was bailing the last of the previous night's drunks. "Where is he, Ted," asked Sam?

There was no sign of anyone the other side of the desk looking remotely like a police inspector. There was an elderly couple waiting for their offspring to be bailed, the duty solicitor waiting for yet another client, a builder waiting to, probably, report the theft of some tools and a young woman.

He ruled her out. She was studying her ipad as she sat waiting. He did wonder what she was doing there as he made his way round the desk and out the door onto the forecourt. There was no one there.

He returned and studied the young woman. He guessed she was in her late twenties. Immaculately groomed and dressed in clearly designer clothing of the most expensive kind. She, to him had the look of the wealthy about her. He dismissed her again and looked around for a contender for a Detective Chief Inspector from Brighton.

"DS Shaw?"

He realised the young woman was addressing him. He turned to see that she had risen from the bench and was talking to him. She was tall with, nearly five feet nine inches and, with her heels, was nearly up to his six foot one. She had dark brown hair, with not one out of place. Her skin was flawless and her face perfectly symmetrical. It was an intelligent face, with dark brown eyes that keenly took in the surroundings. She repeated his name and he saw that the lipstick was perfectly applied to her slightly full lips. She definitely did not look like the sort of person you would expect to find in a run down Nick in a seaside town. She would have fitted better at a luncheon for business women in a high end hotel in central London.

Her voice was what was colloquially called posh. She spoke with minimal movement of her lips and teeth. The vowels were elongated in the manner associated with a good private school education and then a few years at Oxford.

"Can I help you?"

She extended her hand," Mandy Pile."

Sam looked blank, "Who?"

"DCI Piles?" she said.

"DCI," he repeated.

"From Brighton." she was beginning to wonder if he were some sort of simpleton as she watched his brain process the information at the speed of a wooden clock.

"DCI Piles?" he repeated himself. "Sorry, yes, I have been waiting for you."

"Well here I am. Shall we get on with it, or are we going to stand here all day?" As he led her along the corridor and up the stairs, Sam could not help but wonder, what sort of copper she was. It would not take him long to find out.

She was the type of copper that got straight down to it.

"Give me the files. Go home, get some sleep. Come back at two o'clock and I shall have the team sorted by then." He left her to it.

She started to read. Her outward confidence was not quite her inner feelings. This was her first murder, her first real test. Up to now it had all been plain sailing. Sam Shaw's assessment of her had been perfectly accurate, privately educated, Oxford and fast tracked through the ranks. Family connections had also played their part. She knew that she had it in her, but there was always self doubt and the need to prove herself to her colleagues, who were all too eager to brand her a chinless wonder.

Kelly Albright had been murdered at just before nine the previous evening, in a Church car park. Her body, stabbed several times, had been found by Clara Clark when she had returned to her car. She read her interview notes, seen nothing, heard nothing and had only seen the body when she opened the door to her car and the interior light turned on revealing the scene.

Very little was known about the victim so far. According to her fiancé, she had turned up in Eastbourne a few months back and they had met in fast food outlet where she was working. John Draper, it was clear from the interview that he knew little about her. It was a whirl-wind romance and full steam ahead to marital bliss.

She read on. The forensic report would be some while yet and the only thing that was clear was that she had been stabbed. She made a note to interview the Vicar, the reverend Grant and a Matthew Shelly, one of the congregation, that had been arguing.

Having the basic facts to hand, she made her way to see the Super to organise a team and some working space. She knew that they would have to be further officers brought into Eastbourne. That would take organisation and diplomacy. There were three other murder investigations running in Brighton alone and resources were scarce. She knew that the scarcity was why she had been given her chance, despite her lack of experience. She was not in change of the enquiry because of her experience, but because they had no one else available.

She was determines to fight her corner and get the resources she needed as she made her way to the Super's office. Half an hour later she emerged with half of what she had asked for. It would slow matters down and she was well aware that the first few days were crucial in any investigation. Witnesses forgot and physical evidence disappeared the longer the delay. There were only so many hours in a day and the smaller the investigating team was, the more delay there was bound to be in reviewing the evidence. She scheduled the first meeting, allowing enough time for all to be present.

Sam Shaw got the text to wake up and get back to the Station. After his mandatory moan, he got up, showered and headed back to work. He decide he was definitely too old for all this malarkey as he entered the compound at the police station to find that his car parking space had been taken by one of the coppers sent over to help from Brighton. "Give the bugger that's taken my space a parking ticket," he said to the desk sergeant, as he made his way to the incident room.

Chapter 4

"This is DCI Pile, she will be heading up the investigation." Superintendent Taylor addressed the group of officers in the incident room. Along with Mandy and Sam, there were three DC's: Merryweather, Potts, Siskin and a family liaison officer, Constantinou.

Mandy stepped forward to acknowledge the introduction. "Introductions made, I am afraid I have to be somewhere else. I shall leave you to it." Taylor left, looking at his watch. Ten minutes later he was being driven back to Brighton. The austerity and under funding of the last decade by the Government were beginning to cut deep. There were only so many so called efficiency savings to be made. In the end the biggest expense in any enterprise was staff.

"As you know, a young woman, Kelly Albright, was found murdered in the car park of St Andrews. I have provided you all with what witness statements there were. She and her fiancé John Draper, were attending some sort of pre-nuptial Christian induction course. They had been going every Wednesday for the last few months."

The team rummaged through the notes Mandy had provided. She waited patiently while they familiarised themselves with the interviews taken the previous night and the initial medical findings. DC Potts spoke first, having recently moved to plain clothes and being slightly naïve. "Nobody seems to have had an opportunity or a motive."

He hardly had time to compete the sentence before Sam said, "You get that a lot with crimes, nobody ever did it and nobody ever sees anything. Odd isn't it?" There was surprised laughter and a dirty look aimed at Sam from Mandy.

"I want you," she looked at Potts, "and Merryweather to find out everything about the victim. "Siskin and Constantinou, I want you to go through the statements and run background checks on everyone who was at the Church last night. Sam, you and I will interview the fiancé."

"Anything else? we'll meet back here at five."

The drive to the South Harbour development took about ten minutes. Mandy could feel tension between her and DS Sam Shaw as he drove. It did not surprise her. He had spent years in the force and worked his way through the ranks the hard way. From his point of view she had just waltzed in and had gone straight to the top. To make matters worse, her privileged upbringing created a social divide. The widening divide between rich and poor in the Country as a whole had created resentment to those that were now termed the elite.

Mandy was well aware of how she came across. She was not deaf and had heard the term 'posh bitch,' frequently banded about by her colleagues. There was little she could do about her being posh. She knew however, that she was good at what she did and was determined to prove it. Not for her detractors but for herself. Her job was to catch the bad guys and she was going to do it.

John Draper opened the door to the flat. "DCI Pile and DS Shaw," she said as she raised her warrant card for him to inspect. He stepped aside and they walked down the hall to the lounge. The lounge was large with double doors and two windows. They had a vista over the harbour. The doors opened onto a terrace that gave further views to the sea beyond.

"Beautiful view," said Sam.

John nodded in response. He had the demeanour of a man in shock and grieving. Mandy felt that his response was genuine. She looked at Sam, he was clear that he shared her assessment.

The flat was ultramodern with the minimalist look so favoured by the younger generation. They sat on the black and chrome chairs, Sam with his notebook and pen in hand.

"Tell me what happened."

"I told your PC last night."

"I know, but let's just go over everything from the beginning. At this stage we cannot know what is important and what is not. The smallest detail could be crucial."

John explained how they had got ready and drove to the Church.

"You say she deliberately dressed, in your words 'a bit sexy'. What exactly did you mean by that?" Mandy said.

"She was just being a bit rebellious. She thought the whole religious thing ridiculous and said so. It was her way at annoying the rest of the group, perhaps not so much annoy but, as I said, rebel. She was quite independent and did not like to conform."

"And did it annoy anyone in particular?"

"No, I don't think so."

"People can take their religious beliefs very seriously," said Sam.

"Well the Vicar raised an eyebrow."

"The reverend Grant, when you say, 'raised an eyebrow'. What do you mean?"

"He was talking with one of the other members, Matthew. He is the self-important type, about forty. You know probably a virgin with no real life of his own. He was saying how disgusting it was to have these types turning up just so they could get married in Church."

"I am sure that angered you."

"No, not really. The internet is full of trolls and haters. They just sit in their bedrooms watching porn, while preaching at everyone else about morals. Their hypocrisy makes them feel important."

"How did the Vicar react?" said Mandy.

"Well, he seemed to be agreeing."

"And you said nothing?"

"I wanted to, but my parents are very religious and I know how important a Church wedding is to them. I bit my tongue."

"Are you a believer?" said Sam.

"I suppose I am. It is hard to shake off, it sort of stays with you when you are brought up with it."

"Give me a child to the age of seven and I shall give you a Catholic for life," said Mandy. Sam looked at her quizzically, "Ignatius

Loyola," she continued.

"Quite," said John.

"So Kelly left the meeting?"

"Yes, were doing silent contemplation. You sort of stand there with your eyes shut and reflect inwardly on yourself, a sort of meditation. I didn't know she had gone at first. I opened my eyes and saw she had slipped out. I guessed she had gone for a cigarette break."

"Did she do that often?"

"She is trying to quit but the sessions are about two hours, so most weeks she nips out for a fag."

"Did anyone else leave?"

"I am not sure. The Vicar usually goes out and leaves us to it, usually when we are watching a video. He must see them over and over again."

"What about this Matthew Shelly, was he there all the time?"

"I honestly couldn't say."

"Was there anything else you can think of, anything out of the ordinary that happened?"

"No, nothing," he said.

"Now tell me about Kelly, friends, enemies?" said Mandy.

"She didn't really know anyone. We spent most of our time together, with my family or with friends I have known for years."

"Enemies, ex boyfriends?"

John hesitated as he considered the question. "I am not sure, but I did see her email once. She had left it logged on. It was from someone called Jeff. It seemed he was trying to see her or find her. I asked her who he was. She just said some saddo who wouldn't leave her alone."

"Did you follow it up with her?"

"No, not really, she just said it was someone she had once known and wouldn't stop pestering her."

"A sort of stalker?" said Sam.

"Well she never mentioned him again, so I assumed it was all over."

"If it's okay with you, we'll take her laptop and get the tech guys to see if it reveals anything. She didn't have a mobile phone with her. Do you know where it is?"

"No, it doesn't seem to be around," he replied.

They made their way to the car, laptop in hand. "Where next?" said Sam.

"Let's have a word with the Vicar."

Chapter 5

The Church car park was still sealed off with police tape when Mandy and Sam pulled up. There was a group of uniformed officers crawling across the scene of the crime on their hands and knees, bagging everything they found. "Very thorough." said Sam.

"You never know," said Mandy. "The killer may have left something, a cigarette butt with DNA or a tissue."

"Right a dog end or some snot. Does that ever happen in real life?"

"Well, there might be some criminal who has never watched a crime thriller on the telly and kindly left his mark at the scene."

"Right, if he were that stupid the chances are we would have already had the nutter banged up," said Sam. "At the moment it looks like a random killing, in which case it will be a bugger to solve."

"Well let's see if the Vicar can help." They made their way to the vestry.

"I don't think I can help much," said the Reverend Grant. "As I told the officer last night, I didn't really see her leave."

"I understand you had a conversation earlier with a Matthew

Shelly, one of your other parishioners, about Kelly?" said Mandy.

"That was harmless."

"The word, Jezebel and tart, was overheard. Did you share Mr Shelly's view on Kelly?"

"Shall we say that Matthew is quite fundamental in his beliefs? In my experience it is simpler to go along with it rather than debate the issue. He is fond of quoting the bits of the Scriptures that suit his point of view and turning a blind eye to the parts that preach a more tolerant interpretation."

"I see," said Sam, "but you don't feel that it's anything more than bluster?"

"Only God sees what is in men's hearts."

"Quite so Vicar, on a more practical note, we need to know everyone that has come into contact with the victim. I understand that these Alpha courses are more or less run continuously." So what we want to do is look back at who has attended, but were not at last nights meeting, someone who may have come into conflict with the victim in the past for example," said Mandy.

"Well I kept an attendance record if that would help? The Church is now quite strict. You have to do your six months on the course, attend services and then sit down with your Vicar and explore the meaning of marriage. If you do that, you get to marry in Church."

"And then you never see them again until the Christening or funeral?"

"More or less, "the Reverend Grant smiled.

"We'll take the register with us and get it sorted back at the station," said Sam.

"I keep it on my laptop and there's a bit of a problem with my printer," the Vicar hesitated.

"The sooner we get working on the people that came into contact with the victim the better. The first few hours in a murder investigation are always crucial. The longer things are left, the more chance that evidence gets lost or destroyed. We shall take your computer, get the information we need and get it straight back to you,"

"Is that it on the desk?" said Mandy.

"Er, yes."

"No problem," Sam walked over to the desk and disconnected it, and gathered it up along with the charger. "Do you have a password?"

The Reverend Grant was becoming flustered. "I have my sermon and many other Church matters on it. I'd rather you didn't take it."

"Don't worry. The police tech team will download the drives in minutes and we will ensure that it will be dropped back. We will get straight on it. It will be back in two hours, tops." Sam smiled reassuringly.

"Password?" said Mandy.

"Lamb of God, all one word, capital L capital G."

"We'll get it straight back to you," said Mandy as they left the Vestry and made their way back to the car. They handed the Vicar's laptop to a uniformed officer with instructions to take it to the Station.

"Where to now?" said Sam.

"Matthew Shelly, where does he work?"

"He is retired but works in Asda, supermarket."

Ten minutes later Mandy and Sam were sat in the Manager's office in Asda with Shelly sat on the opposite side of the desk. "You were overheard calling Ms Albright a jezebel, then she was found stabbed to death in the car park," said Mandy.

"I had nothing to do with her death. I was in the Church all the time. There were witnesses."

Sam referred to the witness statements taken earlier at the scene. "You left for about fifteen minutes during the silent meditation. That was the exact time Kelly took her cigarette break. Where did you go?"

"To the toilet,"

"You spent the entire fifteen or so minutes in the toilet. You didn't go outside? What took you so long? When asked last night by the Constable you said, I quote, I was only a few minutes, I had a quick pee? In fact it was closer to twenty minutes. I ask again, what took you so long"

Matthew Shelly's face began to redden. He was in his sixties, balding and overweight. A small bead of sweat was forming on his top lip and he began to fidget awkwardly.

"Are you married, Mr Shelly?" Mandy asked.

"No,"

"Have you ever been married?"

Shelly began to squirm further under the gaze of the two police men. "No I have never met the right person."

"Did you find Kelly attractive?" Sam asked.

"Of course not, I would never find such a woman attractive."

"What sort of woman is that?"

"You know what I mean."

"I think I do," said Mandy. "She excited you, didn't she? Did you have thoughts about her, fantasies perhaps?"

Shelly was now becoming increasingly uncomfortable under questioning. "No, I am a good Christian."

"As you keep saying, but the fact is you were absent from the meeting for fifteen minutes when Miss Albright was stabbed to death."

"I wasn't the only one. The Vicar disappeared and got back after I returned from the toilet. Have you asked him what he was doing?"

Sam and Mandy exchanged looks. The reverend Grant had given the impression he had been with the group the entire time.

Driving back to the station, with Sam at the wheel, Mandy spoke. "Well I think we know what he was doing?"

"Having a wank in the toilet while imagining what he was doing with our victim."

"He was condemning her over her scandalous dress while getting off on it in the toilets. However we can't rule out that he was genuine in his disgust of her and decided to murder her either."

"To be honest though, even though the Vicar and Shelly had the opportunity, there was no sign of blood on their clothing," said Mandy.

"Can't rule them out though,"

They pulled into the Police Station car park. "Let's see what the rest of the team have turned up," said Mandy.

Chapter 6

"Well what do we have?" Mandy stood in front of the white board in the incident room. Her team where sat around, notes books in hand. "Let's start with the victim, Kelly Albright. Constantinou, have you contacted the parents about their daughter's death."

"I have not been able to track them down yet."

"There's a good reason for that. Just as you walked in I got a reply from the registry of births, deaths and marriages," said DC Potts. "They are dead."

"How?" said Mandy.

"Car crash but there's more," Potts started to speak as his cell phone rang. "Excuse me I need to take this." He walked to the back of the room.

"Any other relatives, brothers or sisters?" said Sam.

"Only child," replied DC Constantinou.

"Well that makes that simpler," said Mandy. "Keep in touch with the fiancé and provide support." Constantinou nodded her head.

"Background, DC Siskin?"

"There is something on the Vicar. He was at a Church in Sheffield. Where a woman was attacked, raped and murdered."

"On Church premises?"

"No." said Siskin.

"Well the fact that the Reverend Grant was the Vicar at a Church in a city where a murder happened, hardly puts him in the frame for this one," said Mandy.

"I agree," said Sam. "But there was definitely something not right when we spoke to him earlier."

"Did they catch the murderer?"

Siskin replied, "Yes."

"Well that rules out our weird Vicar then," said Sam.

"Except, If you let me finish, it doesn't entirely. The Verger at his Church was convicted of the murder," said Siskin.

Mandy was about to do a double take before speaking. "So he knew the perpetrator, what was his name?"

"Steven Moore, he was sentenced to life."

"So he knew this Steven Moore and would have had regular contact with him. Was there anything linking them, could our Vicar have played a part? Get hold of the files and go through them. Look for anything that might have been missed," said Mandy.

"That has to be too much of a coincidence," said Sam.

"Can I interrupt," said DC Potts.

"Go on."

"Our victim, Kelly Albright, she's dead."

"Er, yeah, we sort of know that Potts, that is in fact the reason why we are all sitting here," said Sam. "It's not that complicated. Someone gets murdered and we, the Police, get together and sort of figure out who did it."

"Very funny Sarge, no I mean, that our victim isn't our victim. Kelly Albright died two years ago in a car crash with her parents," said Potts.

"So who was murdered last night?" said Sam.

"Give me the details of Kelly's death?"

"From what I have just gathered, Kelly Albright was a prostitute and drug user. It seems that her parents came to London where she had been released from hospital following an overdose. Usual story, it seems she had got in with a bad crowd as a kid and made her way from Bristol, where her parents lived, to the Capital. They had heard nothing from her for years. Then they got a call asking for help and decided to drive up to London and get her from a sort of squat or wherever and take her back to Bristol. They had some sort of plan to get her into rehab."

"So what happened?"

"They crashed on the way back on the M4 motorway. They were all killed. They hit a lorry," said Potts.

"So who is our victim?"

"Okay, Merryweather, we have her laptop so it is now a priority that we see if there is any clue as to whom she was," said Mandy. "Get the finger prints from the deceased and see if we get a hit on any data base."

"And given the connection to the murders in Sheffield, do a full forensic on the Vicar's computer."

Chapter 7

The Reverend Grant sat at the front of the pews looking at the Alter. He trembled slightly as he slowly sank to his knees. The light streamed into the darkened interior of the Church. A single shaft of light fell directly on the table before him. He watched as the dust swirling in the beam created a rainbow effect. The particles ebbed and flowed, rising and falling, dancing above the single brass cross in the centre of the Altarpiece.

He tightly screwed his eyes together. The tears were not to be denied and as he opened them, the moisture ran down his cheeks. "Forgive me for I am weak and a sinner." His voice trembled as he prayed.

He rose and stood in front of the Alter and looked around the Church. For the first time, he saw clearly the majesty of the Church over whose congregation he presided. With almost childish innocence, now long lost, he saw anew what he had seen all those years ago when his Mother had taken him every Sunday to evensong.

Then as a child and now as a man, he saw that God dwelt here and that he was here for all men, the good, the bad, the sinner and the saint. It was a real tangible thing to the Reverend. It was something he could feel, he could touch, he could draw strength from. There was only one question he could ask.

"Lord, why did you make your servant this way?"

He rose and laid the wafer on the table and poured wine into the cup. Then, alone, he began to incant. "As we gather at the Lord's Table we must recall the promises and warnings given to us in the Scriptures and so examine ourselves and repent for our sins. We should give thanks to God for his redemption of the world through his Son Jesus Christ and, as we remember Christ's death for us and receive the pledge of his love, resolve to serve him in holiness and righteousness all the days of our life."

The tears ran from his eyes as he listed the sins of the Ten Commandments and as he said the words "Lord have mercy," he knew that he would have no mercy shown to him when his sins were exposed.

"Almighty God, our heavenly Father, who in his great mercy has promised forgiveness of sins to all, those who with heartfelt repentance and true faith turn to him: have mercy on me, pardon and deliver me from all my sins; confirm and strengthen me in all goodness; and bring me to everlasting life; through Jesus Christ our Lord. Amen." He gazed one more time at the stained glass window above the Alter before turning his back and walking from the Church.

The rain began to fall as he left the Church and got in his car. He drove down towards the Sea. He parked and sitting in the car, he looked out across the waves. He felt peace as the sea lapped the shore and the sun broke through the darkening clouds. He knew the time had come and there could be no more delay.

Restarting the engine he drove slowly up the hill away from Eastbourne. He saw the walkers climbing up the hill to the downs, the Children being picked up from School and people drinking coffee in the Café at the foot of the climb to Beachy Head.

As he made his way up the winding road as the rain began to fall in earnest. The sky darkened and the last remnants of sunshine were obliterated by the clouds as the storm rolled in from the sea. The traffic was now all flowing in the opposite direction to him. The wind and the rain had gotten the better of the walkers and sightseers and they hurried from the cliffs and the storm.

There were no other cars left as he pulled into the car park of the Discovery Centre. The rain had become torrential and visibility had been reduced to a few yards with the darkening clouds and almost tropical rain.

He stood beside the car still fully attired in his vestments. The water soaked through and he shivered. He was unclear as to if it was his fear or the cold that caused the trembling. In that moment he felt calm and knew the Lord was showing him the path he must take.

He walked from the car park and crossed the road onto the grass beyond. He walked with purpose and resolve. With every step he came closer to the point where the land would stop, ending in the steep Chalk cliffs that gave way to the sea hundreds of feet below.

"What do you have?" said Mandy as DC Potts walked into her office.

"I have the file on the Sheffield murder."

"And?"

"There seems no doubt that the verger, Steven Moore, was responsible." said Potts.

"Any hint that suspicion fell on our Vicar?"

"It seems just coincidence, wrong place, and wrong time."

"I am not a great lover of coincidences though."

"There is a great similarity in the way the murders were committed but that is all that links ours and Sheffield," said Potts.

"I think we should at least give it a second look. See if we can get to speak to this Steven Moore. Who knows, after spending a bit of time banged up he might want a bit of a chat, even want to unburden himself. See what can be organised," said Mandy. "Gather the troops, I shall be out in a minute to see where we are?"

Potts left and Mandy watched through the glass window of her office as the team gathered around the white evidence board. The board, she had to admit at this stage, was looking very empty. She rose and left her office.

"Okay," she raised her voice to get the teams attention. "Who has something for me?"

"We have the finger prints from the deceased."

"Do we know who she actually is?" said Mandy.

"Nothing, not a sausage," said Sam. "No arrests, no previous, zilch on any database."

"How about her laptop?"

DC Merryweather coughed embarrassingly, "It's proven a bit harder than usual to get into it. We have to do it the hard way. We are copying file by …."

"I'll stop you there, we probably won't understand the technical jargon and I am guessing that the answer is, no progress yet."

"In a nutshell," said Merryweather.

The phone rang, DC Siskin picked it up. He listened and then spoke. "I think you need to put your raincoat on Ma'am."

Mandy said," Am I going somewhere?"

"Beachy Head, they have just found the body of the Reverend Grant. It looks like he jumped off. They found his body smashed onto the rocks at the foot of the cliffs."

Chapter 8

"You seem to be enjoying that cake," said Mandy.

"My wife has me on diet," said Sam. They were sat at a table in the Café at the Birling Gap Visitor's Centre. Sat by the windows it gave them a great view of the sea and the white chalk cliffs. The rain had stopped and the sun was shining.

Mandy took a sip of her coffee and stared for a moment, gazing out to sea in the directions of the so called Seven Sisters cliffs. "You don't like me do you, Sam?"

Sam said nothing and continued to spoon the cake into his mouth.

"You made up your mind as soon as you heard my accent, posh, privileged and pushy?"

"A lot of pee in other words," he said.

"Full of piss in other words."

"I didn't say that."

"No, but that's what you think it. You think that I am here for the ride to the top. You are right to a point. I went to a cosy public school that prepared me for Oxford, then into the Police and fast tracked to Inspector. I am guessing you worked your way up through the ranks?"

"Worked, being the key word," he said.

"But I am doing this for the same reason as you. I have an innate sense of justice. I want to make a difference, catch the criminals and bring them to book. I was sick and tired of reading about young kids being exploited by the drug dealers, girls being prostituted by people traffickers and kids being stabbed and murdered on the streets. I kept saying, why doesn't someone do something? Then it dawned on me that moaning about it was doing nothing. I needed to be the one that did something about it. I am doing this because I want to make a difference."

Sam finished his cake and looked at the elegant young woman sat across the table from him. She looked less like a copper to him than someone who should be sat in Fortnum and Masons having afternoon tea following a rigorous morning of nail varnishing and hair styling. He realised that she was doing her best to establish common ground. He suspected though that she thought of him as a dinosaur, a creature that was on the edge of extinction.

"We don't make a difference, we just slow down the scumbags. They are like weeds. You dig one up and a half a dozen pop up to take their place."

"We can give them a good thinning out though," she smiled.

"Yes, we can do that," he smiled back. He decided he would cut her a little slack. He too had a sense of justice that kept him going in the job for the last thirty years and he wanted the killer of the young girl in the Church car park caught and punished. They would need to work together.

"So what do you think about our Vicar?" They had driven to the Visitor Centre, having spent the last half hour freezing and wet watching the Reverend Grant's body being recovered.

"Not doubt it was suicide. He drove himself up to the cliff and jumped. There is no evidence to show anything else."

"The question remains, why?"

"He has to have murdered the girl, then overcome with remorse, took his own life" said Sam.

"Do you believe that?" said Mandy.

"It would be nice and neat but, no I don't."

"Neither do I. It is true that he was missing from the group at, or around the time she was stabbed..."

"Then there is the murder at his previous Church in Sheffield. I know the verger was convicted but he need not have acted alone," said Sam.

"True, but there are no forensics. He hardly had time to nip out last night, stab her and clean himself up before re-joining the Alpha Class in their meditation. He would be covered in her blood."

"They wear hassocks."

"Cassocks," corrected Mandy.

"Right, they are much like a coverall. Put one on over his jacket and trousers, stab her and then take it off, reappearing in the Hall without so much as a hair out of place," said Sam.

"Hardly likely," said Mandy.

"But possible,"

"Well, if there are blood stained vestments anywhere, the search being conducted, as we sit here enjoying the sea view, will turn them up. I think though, we have to work on the assumption that there was another motive for the murder of the girl we know as Kelly Albright."

"When we find out who our victim really was, we may be a little closer to the motive," said Sam.

"Her laptop may well be the key to that but not knowing anything about the victim, her life, her background, her friends and associates do not make an investigation easy."

"We still need to make sure we rule out our Vicar though. We need to speak to our murdering verger Mr Moore."

Mandy pulled her cell phone from her bag. "Whoops, I received a message when we were up at the Vicars suicide scene. Steven Moore is in Wakefield Prison and he has agreed to an interview."

"Where's Wakefield?" said Sam

"North."

"Bugger, I am guessing I will be taking a train sometime soon."

"Take Potts with you so you don't get lost. He will know how to use an app on his phone to get you from the train station to the prison."

Very funny, hah bloody hah, I'll let you pay then," said Sam as he got up and left Mandy to go to the car park.

"You've already paid. It was self-service, remember?"

"Bugger," said Sam. "Not only have I got to go all the way to bloody Wakefield, I have paid for my own weight gain."

Chapter 9

"Morning team," said Mandy as Merryweather, Potts and Constantinou pulled up their chairs facing her in the incident room. "DS Shaw and DC Siskin, as we speak are making their way to Wakefield prison to interview Steven Moore, Reverend Grant's murdering verger. So who has something to tell us?"

Potts coughed, clearing his throat before proceeding. "We have managed to get into our victims laptop. We are working on the email account. There is nothing of great interest on it, mostly searches for wedding stuff, wedding dresses, catering and venues."

"What is the name on the email account?" said Constantinou

"Racygirl658, not much of a clue to her identity there," replied DC Potts.

"Can we get into it?" asked Mandy.

"Working on it,"

DC Merryweather spoke, "look I have been thinking about this. Our Victim took the name of a known prostitute that was killed in a car crash. We could make the connection that she knew the deceased and that an email address like racygirl is the sort of name an escort might use. Our victim could be an escort."

"Where did Kelly Albright work as a prostitute?" said Mandy.

"Kings Cross area, London," said Merryweather.

"Okay, it looks like you and I are going to do a bit of door to door in that area. Get onto local vice and get all the information on girls working in Kings Cross. You and I will then take a photo of our victim, show it around and see if we can't find out who she is," said Mandy to Merryweather.

Mandy continued, "Potts, we need to get into her email account as soon as possible. Without knowing who our victim really was it will be almost impossible to see why anyone would kill her."

"The Vicar," said DC Constantinou. "We have the report back, it was definitely suicide. The stomach was almost empty, just a trace of wine and a bit of biscuit. It looks like he administered communion to himself before he tidied everything up at the Church, drove to Beachy Head and jumped off."

"Anything at the Church that would give us a reason?" said Mandy.

"Nothing, no suicide note or anything,"

"So one of his parishioners is murdered in the Church car park and within twenty four hours, the Reverend Grant throws himself off Beachy Head. There has to be a connection," said Potts.

"There is the obvious. He killed the victim and overcome with guilt killed himself," said Merryweather.

"Both he and Matthew Shelley left the meeting and had the opportunity," said Potts.

"There would have been some blood on them. You can't stab people without blood flying about. In any event what about motive?" said Mandy.

"The Reverend could easily have changed or have been wearing his cassock. There is still his connection to the murder in Sheffield and his Verger," continued Potts.

"Was there any blood stained clothing at the Vicarage?"

"Yes, but that was from when he came into contact with the dead girl in the car park. The witnesses are sure that when he bid them goodnight, when our victim was still alive, there was no sign of blood on him."

"So for your theory to work Potts, we are looking at the following: The reverend grant follows our victim into the car park where she is smoking a cigarette, stabs her then removes his cassock, which presumably is blood stained and returns to the meeting. He then says goodnight to everyone. Then when the girl's body is found, he returns to the car park and prays while holding the victim and gets blood over himself in the process."

"It is possible though. Look, he leaves the meeting and puts on his vestments. Stabs her, comes in, takes off his cassock and returns in time to see the group off. He waits until the body is discovered, puts on the all ready bloodied clothing and rushes out and comes into contact with the dead girl," said Potts.

"Do we have any witness descriptions as to what our Vicar was wearing when he left them meditating, when he came back and when he arrived at the murder scene?" said Mandy. There was the sound of papers shuffling and mouse clicks as the witness statements were examined by her team.

It was clear within minutes that there was no information on the Vicar's mode of dress the previous evening. That did not surprise Mandy, there was no reason for the officer's taking the statements to ask the question.

"So," said Mandy." Re-interview and find out if the Vicar changed in and out of his vestments and get forensics to look at his clothing and see if they can tell if the blood on his clothing was from stabbing her or from touching the dead body. It is highly unlikely, but we need to rule it out."

"Have we got anything else at this stage?" she continued.

"We have had uniform give us a hand with CCTV. There are not many cameras but there are some. Nothing close to the Church itself but there is one facing the sea front on a hotel which would be the route you would take from the station to the Church and there are cameras at the railway station," said Constantinou.

"And?"

"Nothing really, they focussed on trains leaving after the murder. If the killer came by train, specifically travelling by train to Eastbourne to kill her, he or she would have arrived in the rush home from working in London. There would be too many arriving passengers to pick out anyone, but later, after the murder, the trains are quieter and fewer travellers to look at. What they have been trying to do is pick out some one walking past the hotel CCTV after the murder, who then boards a train and leaves Eastbourne."

"So they are looking at anyone who was in the vicinity of the Church at the appropriate time picked up by hotel and trying to identify them. Then they are looking at departures from Eastbourne by train after she was killed, just in case the killer arrived and left by train. Not much help if they came by car though," said Mandy.

"We are running the registration of all cars picked up at that time that drove along the seafront. There are cameras there but as I said, nothing so far."

"It is a thankless task at this stage. If we had a suspect and a description it would be easier to see if they could be placed at the scene. The other way is just a matter of luck. Okay keep at it, sometimes you can get lucky," said Mandy.

"Anything else?" there was no reply from the team. "So get to it, Merryweather and I will head up to London while you continue the good work here."

Chapter 10

"Will you be dining in tonight, Sir," asked Vera Reynolds.

Raymond Stein sat at his desk in his Mayfair Home, three screens displayed the movements on the various markets analysing and tracking his investments. He had little need these days to leave his home the information technology brought everything he needed right to his front room. There was little need to meet with people. The World now came to him and every day that information made him a little richer. "I will," he replied.

She coughed trying to get his full attention." Will you be alone Sir?"

He paused his activity and focused his attention on Vera. The various markets were now merely a distraction to him, something to entertain him. He had made his money and in reality could not spend it in a hundred lifetimes. He liked to play the game still, but it was no more of a hobby.

"No, I think not. Ask Tim to collect Tracey at eight o'clock and have the Trattoria de Venice to deliver the full works at around nine" he said. "Italian food is her favourite."

"Do you require my presence?"

He smiled, "I'm sure I can manage to serve a few portions of spaghetti."

"If you say so," she said with a note of sarcasm and left him to it.

Tim delivered Tracy at eight thirty. As she removed her coat he said. "Will you need me later, Sir?"

Raymond Stein looked at his newly arrived companion. She smiled seductively in response and made her way to the dining room. "Apparently not," he replied.

She was sat waiting at the table when he followed her into the room. He heard the front door close as Tim made his exit. She had removed her jacket and underneath, she was wearing the sheerest of blouses. He could plainly see her firm breast and erect nipples. "Thank you, see how perfect they are." She wiggled her chest from side to side.

"You were perfect as you were."

"Well thank you anyway. I feel better in myself."

"As long as you don't get addicted to surgery," he smiled.

"No, it was just my breasts. One was larger than the other."

"They're better normal but nice as they are. We still need to discuss the wedding though."

"Raymond I am an escort. That's what I do for a living. I provide a service. It is a job. Men pay me for my time."

"I am aware of that. I merely want to employ you on a full time basis rather than a zero hour's contract," he laughed.

"Look," she said, "I am flattered, I may be a whore but I am not a thief. I would only be marrying you for money. Raymond, I like you but I don't love you …"

"You have no need to tell me. I am old, very old. I am also realistic, I will not live for ever. I am rich and why shouldn't I indulge myself a little before I die?"

"I am a person Raymond not a pet. I don't want to live my life married and at your beck and call."

"I know that. As I said I am a realist. I have my lawyers prepare a contract, fifty million for three years of your life."

She was taken aback, "fifty million pounds?"

"After three years you can walk away or you can stay, for another ten million a year or until either one of us tires of the arrangement."

She sat silent. The figures were incomprehensible to her. She was reasoning that she sold herself for hundreds at the moment, she was doing alright, but fifty million was something entirely different.

"So?"

"Well they say money can't buy happiness.."

"Well they are wrong," he interrupted.

"Okay,"

"You accept?"

"Yes I accept," she said.

He reached into his pocket and pulled out the ring box. "Will you marry me?"

"Yes," she said and he gave her the box.

She opened it. "Oh my God, "she gasped. The single diamond was so large she could hardly believe it to be real. She stood and placed it on her finger. She crossed around the table and kissed him.

She then stood and stripped naked as he watched. "With a ring this size I think that is enough clothing for any girl, don't you," she laughed as she threw her knickers at him.

"There are a few bits of paper to sign though."

She began to undo his shirt. "Let's do it naked."

Having signed the will and the agreement, she slowly lowered herself to her knees and began to fellate him as he signed. "Well it is sort of my signature," he laughed.

He looked at her signature on the documents. "Is that your real name?""It will soon be Mrs Raymond Stein," she smiled.

"Add you date of birth and that can be your access code that I will give to my solicitors. They will hold the money in escrow." Two weeks later she disappeared and despite the efforts of the best investigative agency in London, he could not find her.

Chapter 11

"Did you ever pass a driving test?" said DS Shaw.

"We could have taken the train, if you were that bothered," said DC Siskin.

"I am not long off retirement and I was hoping to live long enough to get my pension. There is a speed limit you know."

"Bit of luck you are not in traffic then. If we are pinged it will come up as a police vehicle."

"I know that but there was no rush. It wasn't an emergency," grumbled Sam.

"It was for me, the Seagulls are playing tonight and I want to get to the match."

"Oh right, I am a lot happier now, that as I lay dying on the motorway that it was in such a noble cause, so you could get home in time to watch eleven blokes kick a football about. Just take it a bit steadier, that's all I am saying."

"Okay sarge," Siskin looked at his watch. "They are taking their time aren't they?"

Sam rolled his eyes in exasperation. "Patience, we are lucky that we are getting to talk to Moore. He doesn't have to agree to anything."

They were sat in a small interview room in Wakefield Prison. They could not help noticing on their arrival that the mostly Victorian buildings had seen better days. It was tired, overcrowded and understaffed. The Governor, a man in his late fifties, had the look of someone who had just about had enough. Lack of funds and staff meant that his job had reduced to papering over cracks. The prison was awash with drugs and violence among the prisoners was on an upward trajectory.

"He is one of the more rational ones," said the Governor on meeting Shaw and Siskin. "Most are dangerous sex offenders and disturbed. We don't have the resources to help them. We just contain them. A lot of them would benefit from psychiatric care not prison, but we are the cheaper option."

"It's the same with the Police, believe me. We spend a lot of time dealing with depressed and mentally ill people. We are not the right people for the job. Night after night we end up with people in the cells that should be in hospital for their and other people's safety," said Shaw.

"This Steven Moore, is he rational?" said Siskin.

"More than most," replied the Governor. He looked down at the file on the desk in front of him. "He's essentially a sociopath. He's bright, articulate and highly manipulative, so be warned. He will take advantage of any situation. Do not rely too much on what he tells you."

The door opened to the interview room and Moore entered accompanied by one of the guards. He studied Shaw and Siskin before walking round the table and taking the seat opposite. He spoke first, "to what do I owe this pleasure?"

"My name is DS Shaw and this is DC Siskin and we should like to talk to you about your time in Sheffield."

"Have you found her then?"

Siskin's jaw fell open. Before he could betray their astonishment further, Sam spoke, "Yes, but we need your help and that is why we are here."

A look of satisfaction spread across the verger's face. "You need my help, but do I want to help, that is the question?"

Sam looked at Siskin signalling to keep his peace. He knew from experience that the man facing them enjoyed being in control. Moore felt he was superior and that the policemen were below his intellectual level. If he told them anything, it was because he wanted to demonstrate how clever he was and how stupid they were. He would not respond to questioning if he felt he was not getting the respect he was due.

"We admit it," said Sam. "We are stumped we need your help?"

"Do you know who she is?" smirked Moore.

Not even aware there was a further victim other than the one Moore had been convicted of, Sam needed to think fast. "Decomposition is the factor," he said vaguely.

"I can't help you. I never really knew who she was. I saw her about. She bunked off school a lot and hung out at the kebab shop, drinking. She was a bit of a slut."

"That would be the kebab shop on?"

"Wicker,"

Sam could see the light of realisation going on in Siskin's brain. For years there had been systematic grooming of young girls in Rotherham. A group of seven men have been found guilty of grooming and exploiting young girls, including one who was sexually abused by at least a hundred Asian men before the age of sixteen. They were brought to trial in Sheffield.

It was clear that Moore had committed a further murder that no one had been aware of. Sam now knew that there was a missing girl's body somewhere. He also knew that somehow, he needed to find out from the man in front of him where the body was.

"Do you remember the..."

"The murder?" a smile of satisfaction spread across Moore's face as he recalled the details. Siskin felt like smashing his smug face in. Sam frowned at him. Siskin realised he was losing control and forced his expression back to that of nonchalance.

It was clear that the man opposite was becoming sexually aroused as he recounted the death of the young girl. He was speaking faster and faster as he told the details.

"She was off her face, booze and pills. She had been to a party with a couple of other girls. I met her by pure chance. I had been at the Church and was on my way home. I was on Wicker and was going to get some fried chicken. I needed a piss and went round the back of some shops." He paused while he replayed events in his mind. "There were always a lot of Asian men hanging around that area."

"Now we know why," said Siskin barely disguising his disgust. Sam gave him another reprimanding looking. He needed to be quite and let Moore talk.

"Yeah the little sluts were putting out for them. They loved it, the slags." Sam nodded his approval encouraging Moore to continue. He noticed that the guard standing behind Moore was sickened by the man. He suspected that Moore might well have some form of mishap on the cell block when they left.

"Anyway, she just walks up to me and asks if I have any coke?"

"So you said yes," said Sam.

"I say I do but that we need to go somewhere quiet where we can fuck and then I'd give her the coke."

The silence hung heavily in the air. They knew that this was the crucial point. They waited tensely, not wishing to break the mood. At that point Moore paused and looked around as if coming to the realisation that he was about to confess to a murder. The anticipation was palpable.

Sam feared that Moore was about to clam up. He needed to do something. Fighting his anger and revulsion he spoke hoping to revive Moore's mood of sexual excitement. "So you fucked the slut? I bet she loved it. Did you fuck her right there, up against a wall?"

Now believing that Sam was a kindred spirit he continued. "I took her back to the Church Yard. I fucked her in the grave yard. When I finished she wanted her reward. I didn't have any coke of course and told her fuck off. She started shouting the odds. I don't know who she thought she was the slag?"

"Too right," said Sam encouraging him further.

"I started to shut her up. She just kept struggling. So I smashed her head into a headstone. There was blood everywhere. I found a small fork. Someone must have left it after they tended to a grave. You know. the type of thing they use for planting flowers. Anyway, I suddenly had it in my hand. I started stabbing her with it."

It was clear that Moore was becoming more and more sexually agitated as he recalled stabbing the young girl to death. Sam and Siskin could plainly see how dangerous and deranged this man was as he revelled in reliving the gory details of her death.

"And that is how her body ended up..?"

"In the grave that was being dug that day," he said.

Sam sat patiently, "just one thing, the Vicar, Reverend Grant, did he get involved?"

Moore looked confused, "that Wanker?"

Chapter 12

"DI Pile and this is DC Merryweather," said Mandy

"Pleased to meet you both. I am DS Singh. People call me Danny." They were sat in the police station local to Kings Cross, gathered around his desk. Danny already had Kelly Albright's criminal history displayed on his computer terminal. The room was busy with about fifteen coppers working and chatting.

"Is it always like this?" said Merryweather.

"Yes, it is a bit quiet today, nobody stabbed or murdered for a few days now," said Danny.

Mandy laughed. "So what can you tell us about this Kelly Albright?"

"Not much more than is on the data base."

"But you have come across her personally?" said Merryweather.

"Yes I picked her up a few times for soliciting, not that we always charge them. The focus is more on the people traffickers these days. Organised gangs from Eastern Europe bring in girls and trade them as money making commodities. Kelly was your run of the mill working girl, got in with the wrong crowd as a kid, abused at home, ran away to

London, acquired a pimp, a heroin addiction and forced onto the street."

"Are you sure about the abusive home life? Weren't her parents taking her to rehab when they were all killed in a car crash?" said Mandy.

"Sorry, I was being generic. For whatever the reason she ended up being pimped on the London streets. Perhaps the drugs came first in Bristol, where she grew up, or perhaps she meets the wrong sort of bloke who turned out to be a pimp," said Danny.

"Did she have a pimp?"

"Mantis Canous, Latvian, no longer with us I am afraid. He seems to have got himself the wrong side of the wrong sort of people. He was stabbed to death outside a pub about eighteen months ago. He was a total scumbag. so no great loss to anyone. We never found out who was responsible."

"Do you know how she ended up in the car with her parents the day it crashed?"

DS Singh began to rummage through the notes in the paper file he had retrieved from the archives. "The traffic investigation report on the screen doesn't go into that," he said.

"So we don't know exactly how she ended up being driven back with her parents or how they found her?" said Mandy.

"Hold on, I am trying to find a log from a few days earlier. I sort of remember something about…" He stopped speaking as he dug through the bits of paper.

Mandy and Merryweather sat patiently waiting as he looked,

"Ah here it is. I knew there was more, right, two days earlier there was a 999 call. The caller said she had overdosed and gave an address. The ambulance crew found her, gave her a Naloxone injection and got her to Archway Hospital."

"Who made the call?"

"They didn't give a name?"

"Is there a record of the phone number," said Mandy.

Danny looked through the call log and finally located it. "I am tracing it now, hang on." There was a wait of about five minutes while contact was made. "Okay, it was registered to Kelly. Looks like the caller used her phone to call for the ambulance."

"I was hoping that the caller was the girl that had just been murdered in Eastbourne and that she might have called."

"It's logical. Whoever took Kelly's identity must have known her well and have had access to her ID and NI number," said Danny.

"And knew that she had died," added Merryweather.

"Life is never that easy. In an ideal World our dead girl would have been the one to find Kelly and used her cell phone to call for an ambulance. The phone would have given us our victim's name, address and bank account details before she took Kelly Albright's identity," said Mandy.

"Do you recognise her by any chance?" said Merryweather, giving Danny the photograph taken of the deceased at the morgue.

He looked at it, thinking for a while. "No, I am sorry. I just can't recall seeing her."

"We could try and ask some of the girls on the street. Show her photo around," said Mandy.

"Kelly was killed nearly twenty two months ago now. That is a long time on the Streets around here. Faces come and go. The girls move from town to town now. They advertise on the web saying they will be in town for a few days and the punters book them. Then they move on. It keeps the meat fresh, so to speak. The old days of hanging about on street corners are all but gone. You use an app and a phone to get a girl now. That way, no one gets nicked for curb crawling and the locals aren't plagued by girls hanging around day and night outside their houses," said Danny.

There was silence as Mandy reflected on it. "There must be some way to find out who our murder victim was?"

"TV and press?" said Danny.

"We are heading that way, but releasing details before we know who or what we are dealing with is two edged. It has only been twenty four hours. I should like to know more before we involve the public. We are shooting in the dark at the moment. There is no way we can evaluate what information we get from an appeal. We could be sent off in totally the wrong direction, spending hours of valuable police time following up every bit of garbage we get tipped off about."

"I get that, but your options seem limited at this stage."

"I have two questions I would like an answer to, apart from our victim's identity," said Mandy. "How did she know that she was dead and how did she come into possession of Kelly's ID?"

"She could have read of the crash in the newspaper or heard it on the news," said Merryweather.

"True, but there are lots of crashes and they don't make a big splash. The names of the fatalities are usually withheld to give us the time to break the news to relatives and by the next day they are no longer news. But say our victim did hear it on the news, how did she get Kelly's ID? We have to assume she had her bits and pieces with her when her parents picked her up. Do you have a list of what was in the car and what was on the bodies of her and her parents?"

Danny tapped at the computer before replying. "Well, her parents had the usual, credit cards, driving licenses, keys and money."

"And Kelly?"

"Keys, money but no form of ID, she was identified positively from her fingerprints and criminal record.

There was silence. "Are you thinking what I am thinking?" said Mandy.

"Our murder victim was in the car when it crashed?"

Chapter 13

DCs Potts and Constantinou had been sat in the anti-room for nearly forty five minutes waiting to interview the Bishop. "How do you address a Bishop?" said Constantinou

"What?" said Potts.

"I said, how do you address a Bishop?"

"What are you on about?"

"Well, is he an Excellency, a Grace, a Lord or what?"

"Does it matter?"

"It does if you're a Christian. I don't want to annoy one and mess up my chances of a place in heaven," she smiled.

"Are you a Christian? You're Greek aren't you?"

"I am British, my parents were Cypriot you half wit. Even if I were Greek, what do you think we have as a state religion, Zeus-ism?"

"What's Zeus-ism?

"You are a halfwit. Zeus was the father of the Greek gods. It was a joke."

Potts replied, "Oh yeah, I saw a film about that. I thought that was just legend and stuff though. So that is what Greeks believe then?"

"Do you have any other interests apart from computer gaming and tech?"

"I don't usually leave the Nick, you know that. I have very limited experience of interviewing people. As you say, I spend most of my time forensically examining people's computers in the lab. It is only because we are so understaffed that they put me on this case. I have forgotten most of the stuff they taught us about interview techniques and detection. So there is no need to take the piss."

"I was only joking. Don't take it to heart. I am supposed to be a family liaison officer, but we are a bit short on the family at the moment so it is all hands to the pump."

Well at least you talk to people regularly. That is really not my strong point. I am a geek and I freely admit it," said Potts.

"Greek Orthodox," said Constantinou.

At that point the Bishop's secretary appeared. "The Right Reverend, the Lord Bishop will see you now. Please follow me."

"Well that answers that," said Potts as they followed him down a corridor to the Bishops Office.

They were surprised that the Bishop was a man in his mid-forties. Their expectations were of someone considerable older. "How can I help you?" He had a gentle sing song tone of voice that the clergy seemed to adopt with the public. Potts wondered if there was a module at Seminary College specifically called, 'Calm Voice to Address the Congregation'.

"We would like to talk about the Reverend Grant at Eastbourne," said Constantinou.

"Yes, a very sad business…"

"Quite, did you have any warning that he may have intended to take his own life?"

"We in the Church have available a range on Counselling services available to the clergy, not only faith related but in the wider sense of mental well being."

"Did he avail himself of any of the services?"

The Bishop looked at the file in front of him. "No, he never raised any issues." Potts could not help but notice that the file was very thick.

"So as far as you are concerned, there was no indication as to why he would take his own life, no warning signs, nothing at all?" said Constantinou.

"Nothing,"

"We believe he was at a Parish in Sheffield before being moved to Eastbourne. Was there any reason why he was transferred?"

There was a note of hesitancy in the reply. "These matters are of course internal but we felt that a change would be good for Reverend Grant."

"Why was that?" Constantinou pressed, adding belatedly," My Lord." The interjection was not lost on the Bishop. Constantinou was issuing a timely reminder that he was a vicar of God and duplicity and misdirection was not what you would expect from a high ranking cleric.

There was significant pause before the reply. Even Potts picked up on the hesitation and looked at Constantinou queryingly. The Bishop coughed and then spoke. "There were certain matters that we needed to look into, but the Church was fully satisfied and it came to nothing."Constantinou pressed. "What were these matters, exactly?"

"As I said, they were purely ecclesiastical in nature."

"We would like to be the judge of that, not the Church. Was it to do with Steven Moore and the murder of a young woman?"

"No, of course not, far from it, as I keep saying it was an internal matter."Constantinou was becoming frustrated with the Bishops stone walling and it was beginning to show. Potts, despite his self acknowledged lack of people skills, realised that matters were rapidly escalating.

"I think that is all for now. We thank you for seeing us," he intervened. Constantinou gave him an annoyed glance. He ignored her and got to his feet and proffered his hand to the Cleric. Reluctantly she stood and followed his lead by shaking the Bishops hand before being shown out by his secretary.

Walking back to the car she was still angry. "He was just giving us the run around. You know that don't you?"

"Yes I do," said Potts." But nicking a Bishop for obstruction was not going to solve anything, was it?"

She was regaining her temper. "I hate being lied to and it is worse when it is someone who really shouldn't. It's bloody hypocritical. It gets my goat, that's all."

"You should look up stuff on the web like we nerds do."

"Why is that?"

"Well you would have made the link to the last Bishop this guy replaced about twelve months ago."

"Well?"

"Well you would have made the connection to his trial. He was convicted of paedophilia and covering up for a whole gaggle of child molesting vicars going back thirty years," said Potts

She got in the drivers position and started the engine. "So what do you think he was hiding?"

"We need to look at it from his point of view. He may be hiding nothing. He had been put in as the new broom to clean up the Churche's reputation. It has come under heavy criticism for its handling of these matters in the past. Now there is a renewed determination to shine a light in the dark nooks and crannies. They are determined to stop the old habit of brushing things under the carpet."

"Well he seemed less than forthcoming."

"As I said, look at it from his point of view. No sooner does he seem to have matters under control then there is a murder at a Church in Eastbourne and the Vicar tops himself soon after. He probably doesn't have a clue what is happening, but he must be thinking the worst."

"So you don't think he is withholding evidence?"

"He may be but more likely I think there is a furious activity behind the scenes as the Church throws everything they have at it to get to the bottom of the matter. They are just making sure they have all the facts before releasing the information and calling the police in."

"In other words, watch this space," said Constantinou.

"When they know, I am pretty certain we will be told,"

"Frustrating though,"

"God moves in mysterious ways and the Church even more so," smiled Potts.

Chapter 14

"This is very inconvenient, we have better things to do with our time, you know."

"I do realise that and I am truly sorry for the trouble but it is a murder investigation," said Mandy putting on her best smile and Oxford accent. "Everyone has said how important you are in the smooth running of the hospital and so we have naturally come to you."

Placated and flattered, the Admissions Secretary at the North Middlesex Hospital settled down to look through the staff rota. Now that Mandy and Merryweather had recognised her importance, she now treated them as her new found confidants. "Without me, you know this place would never meet any of its targets. It is people like me that keep the NHS running. All these so called consultants don't know their elbow from their backsides. You would think they were God by the way they carry on." She continued to explain why she was more important to the Hospital than everyone else as she checked the files on the computer.

Merryweather rolled his eyes to the heavens as they listened to the secretary extolling her importance. Mandy gave him a stern look, cautioning him to keep calm. She knew a jobsworth when she met one. They had an opinion on everything and were always right. You challenged them at your peril. If you pricked their pomposity they would become as obstructive as their small amount of actual power would permit. She needed the information this woman could give her and she had no desire to end up seeking court orders and arguing about medical confidentiality.

"Kelly Albright you say?"

"That's right," said Merryweather.

"I have her records, takes an expert to track down anything on this system you know."

"And we are lucky that you are here to help," Mandy said at her most sycophantic.

The secretary beamed with self-importance. "She spent two days on the ward and was discharged." Merryweather made a note of the exact time and dates in his note book.

"We are really interested as to who visited her," said Mandy?

"We don't keep records of that."

"I was hoping to get details of who was working on the ward and interview them."

The woman exhaled to signifying what a big task that would be. It reminded Mandy of a builder pricing a job. She was half expecting her to say, "that will cost you." Instead she began to tap at the keyboard.

"I hope you appreciate this," she said as the ward rota appeared on her screen.

"Would it be possible to have a printout of that?" said Merryweather.

She rolled her eyes as if the task was equivalent to Moses

parting the Red Sea. With just a few more loud exhales, he finally had the printout in his hand.

"We won't take up anymore of your valuable time," said Mandy as they made their escape from her office.

"What a pompous old bag," said Merryweather.

"That's a bit sexist," warned Mandy.

"Cow would have been sexist, bag is non-binary," said Merryweather.

"She means well," said Mandy.

"If you say so,"

There terraced house just off Archway Hill was divided into flats. Merryweather asked the taxi to wait as Mandy rang the doorbell. After several attempts at buzzing, the intercom at the side of the door crackled and a sleepy female voice answered. Merryweather paid the taxi that then drove off. The cooperation of the Metropolitan Police only went so far and it did not run to chauffeuring a couple of provincial plods about. They had offered to make the follow up inquiries on Mandy's behalf but she wanted to move as soon as possible. She and Merryweather had booked into a Premier Inn the previous night and decided to track down the staff on duty when Kelly had been admitted themselves.

On entering the flat they were greeted by a, somewhat bleary eyed, female nurse in her late forties. She explained that she was on nights, hence the fact that she was sleeping so late.

"We are sorry to wake you," said Mandy. "We would like to ask you about a patient on the ward about eighteen months ago."

"You are joking aren't you? I can hardly remember who's on the ward now we are so short staffed. We don't have time to hang about chatting to them."

"Would you just look at a couple of photos and tell us if anything comes to mind," said Merryweather, as he passed across a photo of Kelly taken from her arrest file and the picture of their unknown victim taken at the mortuary.

The nurse got up and fetched a pair of reading spectacles from her handbag sitting on the table to one side of the room. She returned, sitting on the chair opposite the two police officers who were parked on a sofa. The flat was crowded, cluttered and small. A nurse's pay got you very little space in the Capital,

She studied the two photographs for a moment. "I vaguely recall this woman," she pointed to the photo of Kelly Albright.

"And the other girl?"

"Sorry no."

"She may have been a visitor," said Mandy.

"She just does not ring a bell."

Back in the taxi, Mandy spoke first. "This is really not going to be easy. We don't even know if our victim was at the hospital at all. We are just assuming that she was in that car crash."

"Come on, it is the most likely explanation how she ended up having Kelly's ID and documents."

"She could have known where she lived or something and just stolen them or even bought them off someone," said Mandy.

After another two fruitless visits, two overworked nurses and a huge cab fare bill, they were no further on. "Two left on the list," said Merryweather as they approached a council tower block on an estate in Enfield.

They buzzed the door and announced themselves. The door opened and found that the lift was out of order, there were thirteen floors worth of steps to climb. By the time they reached the door of the next interviewee that were quite breathless.

A large black woman opened the door and laughed as they entered, still panting from the climb to the thirteenth floor. "Keeps you fit living here," she said. "The lift has been broken for months."

She put a cup of coffee down on a table in front of them without asking if they wanted it. "Now what can I do for you. I hope it's not that waste of space I married. I haven't seen him in years if you are looking for him?"

"No, it has nothing to do with you or your waste of space," smiled Mandy. "We are trying to find out about someone you treated on the ward." She put the photo of Kelly on the table.

"That's Kelly," she said.

"You remember her?"

"Of course, she was from Bristol. That's where I was brought up. I lived in St Paul's and she was brought up in the posh bit, in Redcliffe. She had overdosed and had a real problem with heroine. You would have thought it would have been the other way around, giving where we lived, me in dope central and her in designer land."

"So you spoke to her, do you remember anything else?"

"I met her parents. They came and got her. They were a bit posh, but they obviously wanted to help. The father got her straight into a rehab facility, somewhere near Bristol and when she was discharged, they were taking her straight there."

"Do you recognise this girl?" Merryweather put the morgue picture of their victim in front of her.

"Oh Jesus, she's dead?"

"She was murdered..."

"Oh no, she was such a cheery girl and so supportive of her friend. I can't believe she was murdered."

"You saw her at the hospital?"

"She was there almost the whole time with Kelly."

"Do you remember Kelly being discharged?" said Mandy.

"Yes, they all left together, Kelly, her parents and her friend. Kelly and I were going to keep in touch but she never texted or phoned and I got no reply to my texts."

"She was killed along with her parents in a crash later that day on the M4."

There was shocked silence.

Mandy had to ask one more question," Did you get the name of her friend?"

"Christine,"

"Surname?" said Merryweather.

There was silence as the nurse thought. She got up and went to a drawer in the kitchen just off the sitting room. They watched her rummage through a pile of papers she had pulled out and dumped on the side. She finally returned with a card.

"I don't know her surname but she ordered some flowers for her friend at the hospital. Kelly gave them to me to take home when she left. We usually leave them on the ward for the next patient, to keep the place looking cheerful. I liked the card that came with them so I took it with me."

She handed a card across with a picture of a smiling cartoon elephant on it. "My boy loves elephants so I took it home for him to look at. He's at school at the moment."

Mandy picked up the card.

"It has a reference and bar code on it." she continued. "I assume that you can trace back the order at Moon Pig and from there you can get Christine's credit card details and so on."

"You are a very smart woman," said Mandy.

"I know that. It is just a pity the NHS doesn't agree with us and pay me more."

Chapter 15

The incident room was a hive of activity when Mandy called them to order. "Pay attention, we have a lot to get through and then you can get back to what you were doing. Sam?"

Sam stood up and made his way to the head of the room. "As you know DC Siskin and I took the brave step and ventured north of Watford to interview Steven Moore at Wakefield Prison."

He continued checking his note book. "He has been convicted of the murder of a young woman. He was, at the time of the murder, the verger at a Church where the Reverend Grant was the vicar. There was no connection made between the two men at the time of the murder, but now that a second murder has occurred, we are investigating any link. I will give you over to DC Siskin who made a note of the interview with Mr Moore."

Siskin stood up and began to recount the interview. He finished by saying, "In summary, Mr Moore admitted a further killing to us during the course of the interview." He resumed his seat at his desk.

"Have we been in contact with Sheffield serious crimes?" asked Mandy.

Sam replied. "We have, but they are, of course, dubious as to the veracity of Mr Moore's claims. He is, of course, mentally unstable and it is difficult to establish what is fact and what is fantasy? On the face of it, the circumstances seem to hang together but they have no reports of a missing girl at that time."

"She need not have come from that area?" said Mandy. "Kids end up all over the Country, especially if they are taken into care."

"To be fair we have done all we can. I have passed on the information to the local coppers. It is their case, not ours."

"I believed him," said Siskin," for what that's worth."

Sam sighed. "We cannot chase down every case in the Country. We have to leave it to the local force."

"Reluctantly we have to leave it, but did you get any sort of link between our suicidal Vicar and the murdering verger?" said Mandy.

"No not really," said Sam.

"He did have a very low opinion of the Vicar though. He called him a Wanker," said Siskin.

"Right, colourful but it doesn't get us much further. Potts and Constantinou tell us about your time with the Bishop," said Mandy.

"One word," said Potts, "evasive."

"I agree. There was clearly something he wasn't telling us," said Constantinou.

"He had an answer for everything and told us nothing. The Church clearly moved Grant away from Sheffield to Eastbourne for a reason, but he made it sound like a routine transfer, I am not buying it," said Potts.

"Look, if we believe Moore, he was clearly on the fringes of the grooming scandal in that area. He was associated with our dead Vicar. It doesn't take much of a leap of faith to put the two together."

"Okay," said Mandy taking the floor. "What we have is a girl, as yet unidentified, murdered in a Church car park, the Vicar with a dubious past, possibly party to a previous murder or at least linked in someway to the grooming of young girls. The victim has, for some reason, concealed her past and her identity. We know she was a close friend of a prostitute whose identity she assumed."

Sam spoke. "It all seems to be tying together, but the how is unclear. We need some theories and further lines of enquiry."

"My gut feeling is that the Bishop is doing a clean up job for the Church. On the one hand they are publicly sending the message that they have cleaned up their act and have stopped covering up for sex offending clerics, while on the other they are playing a damage limitation game and keeping the lid on more sex scandals involving their priests," said Potts.

"Let's just speculate," said Mandy. "Let's for the moment take the viewpoint that our victim had something to hide. She assumes another identity and moves away from London to sleepy Eastbourne. All goes well. She gets a job, meets John Draper and they get engaged."

"All is fine until his parents insist on a Church wedding and she is forced to attend the Alpha classes run at St Andrews by the Reverend Grant," she continued. "Then she recognises someone from her past."

"She could be a threat in two ways. We know she had little money of her own. She could have tried to blackmail someone..."

"Or they were just fearful and acted preventively on the

perceived threat. She may not have even recognised them"

"We need to know more about our victim. But it is clear that no one goes through the trouble of changing their identity without a good reason, but we cannot assume that it was someone at the Church that murdered her. She was hiding from someone. He or she could have tracked her down and disposed of her."

"We have two suspects at the Church, the Vicar who committed suicide and the other absentee from the Alpha class, Matthew Shelley. We need to know more on both of them and, in particular, any links to our victim," said Potts.

"Merryweather and I have made a bit of progress in establishing who the girl masquerading as Kelly Albright actually was. We now know that she was a close friend. We know that she visited Kelly in hospital. We suspect that she was in the car when it crashed killing Kelly and her parents. We think that is when she took Kelly's ID and left the scene to start her new life in Eastbourne," said Mandy.

"Further lines of enquiry," said Sam. "Potts, we need to get into our victims computer and the reverend Grants. Get on it." He looked down at his notes before continuing. "Siskin, we have details of a bunch of flowers and a Moon pig card sent by our victim to Kelly when she was in hospital. Track down the credit card details of the sender. It could give us her true identity. There was no sign of the victim's phone at the scene, we need to find it."

Mandy spoke. "Merryweather, we need to look at the fatal crash that killed Kelly and her parents. Go over the accident report and check if there is any motorway CCTV of the incident. Check service station footage. Let see if the car stopped for petrol by checking Kelly's parent's credit card activity. If they did, check the footage from the services, perhaps they stopped for food or went inside to use the toilets. We need to know for certain who was in that car."

The meeting broke up and Sam wandered into Mandy's office. "Are you buying it?" he said.

"To a point, I believe she stole Kelly Albright's identity and she was hiding in Eastbourne. I don't see the Vicar as a murderer who then committed suicide and Matthew Shelley does not seem to have any motive to kill her. So we are looking at the possibility that someone tracked her down and killed her in the car park."

"Or a random killing?" said Sam.

"A serial killer? It might be. It seems unlikely, but search, the Police National Database. Make use of HOLMES, that algorithm to spot cases that might be linked."

Sam muttered to himself as he left, "algorithm my arse."

Chapter 16

Potts sat at his desk looking blankly into the middle distance. He had been liaising with the computer forensic team all morning, trying to gain access to their victim's email account. Having failed to crack the password, they were waiting on the provider to give them access. Had the dead girl been a suspected terrorist the process would have been far simpler and they would have the information they needed.

It appeared that it would be another twenty four hours or so before the email account provider would let the police access her personal data. Potts was less than impressed with the moral stance being adopted regarding privacy by the giant internet company, given the industries love of selling data to all and sundry.

"Are we getting anywhere with the Reverend Grant's or our dead girl's laptops?" said Mandy, as she approached.

"Bunch of hypocrites, they are seeking legal advice before releasing personal data. It pisses me off. We are investigating two dead people and they carp on about privacy. These are the same arseholes that leave kiddie porn up and let mass murderers stream their killings live, while at the same time selling user's data to foreign governments so they can interfere in democratic elections."

"Not much we can do. We have to abide by the law while they make the law up as they go along," said Mandy. "Just do what you can.

The sooner we can crack their communications the better."

"Have you thought any further about releasing a picture of the dead girl to the media?" he asked.

"Yes, we will have to do it. It is just the lack of resourses that is delaying it. We need enough trained staff to man the phone lines and monitor the outcome. Then there is the problem of investigating the leads generated. There is just a total shortage of coppers. It could all have been so much easier if she had been in the Database."

She walked off. Potts sat staring at the image of the dead girl. He went through the information in his mind of what he had on the victim, which was virtually nothing, other than she had moved to Eastbourne, assumed the identity of a dead girl, an addict and a prostitute. It was logical, he decided, that the deceased might well have been engaged in the same type of activity.

He was soon busy running a facial recognition programme. He started the routine running with a basic search of all escort and swinging advertisements. Given the murder took place in Eastbourne, he initially narrowed the parameters to Eastbourne and Brighton. In theory, if the victim had a photo on the web it should find her. He sat back and waited.

Sam had finished talking to Moon Pig, the internet sender of greetings cards. They recognised the coding on the card and the flowers that had been sent to Kelly Albright in hospital, by the dead girl. The only problem was finding the right person to access the historical data. They were sure they could come up with a name, but they did not keep card details on file unless they had the card holder's permission, in accordance with the data protection legislation. "Okay," said Sam." Get me the name, the date of payment and transaction reference. I should be able to get the card owner's details from the Credit Card provider once I have their reference."

"Well?" said Mandy, having made her way across the incident room from Potts' desk.

"We are getting somewhere at last."

"You will have the same problem as Potts is having with confidentiality even when you get the transaction details."

"They usually are very helpful working closer with the Police on card fraud and stuff. So I should be able to get the information within the hour. The flower supplier just wants to be one hundred per cent certain they give us the right details. They don't have the same resources as the banks do to deal with these matters. That's all."

"Got something," Potts shouted across the room..

Sam got up and followed Mandy across to his desk.

"Look at this," he said, turning his computer screen towards them.

"What's this? Brighton Gangbang?" she asked.

On the screen was an advertisement in the form of a poster. There was a date advertising a monthly event in Brighton. It was headed Brighton Greedy Girls, Anna, Colleen and Mandy, two parties at 1 pm and at 7 pm. Anna will be offering DP and Mandy DVP at this event, £80. Get your ticket and a web address was provided.

"What are DP and DVP?" said Sam.

Potts looked a little uncomfortable. "Double penetration and double vaginal penetration," he eventually volunteered.

"How did you know that?" said Sam.

Mandy stepped in to cover Potts' embarrassment. "Apart from the fact that one of the girls has the same name as me why are you showing us this?"

He scrolled down and there was a poster for a gangbang party in Eastbourne the following week. "I ran facial recognition on escort adverts in and around here. Look at the pictures of the girls," he prompted.

Sam and Mandy lent forward and studied the three topless girls on the poster. "I am not seeing it," said Sam.

"Look at the girl in the purple wig holding the cane?"

"That could be our victim," said Mandy.

"It's a ninety-nine per cent certainty," said Potts. "The pictures of the dead girl taken at the morgue show her face from multiple angles making it much easier to extract the measurements and test for a match."

"We need to trace the organisers and hopefully find her details."

"I am already on it," said Potts.

Sam's phone rang and he returned to his desk to take the call. He sat and began to write. He put the phone down.

"We have a name for the sender of the flowers to Kelly Albright in hospital, Christine Marstone."

Chapter 17

Sam and Mandy pulled up on the industrial estate. The most prominent business was a double glazing manufacturer and two car repairers. About two hundred yards down the road were the Eastbourne Police car depot. "Easy if we need back up," said Sam as they passed the yard full of blue and white police cars.

"Talk about hiding in plain sight," said Mandy, as Sam brought the car to a halt in the yard.

"This is it unit seven, Happy Girls Escorts," he said as they got out of the car.

There were a number of buzzers outside the block of serviced offices. Most had labels over the buttons apart from one. Sam pressed it.

"Who is it?" a female voice came over the intercom by the door.

"Police, open the door," he said. There was a load buzz and a click as the front door unlocked. They entered. There were two offices on each of the three stories. "If you stay here, I'll do some door knocking."

Mandy stood in the doorway while Sam knocked. "Boss," he called down after several minutes, "top floor."

She made her way up the two flights of steps and saw Sam and a middle aged woman at the opened door to one of the offices, "Happy Girls Escorts," said Sam as they followed the woman in. The area was sub divided into two rooms. The first had a table with four chairs around it and a phone system.

"At night there are more of us in here," said the woman, who Sam had established was called Lisa. "I usually come in during the day and sort out the paperwork and bills from the previous night with the boss, Mr Vasilescu. As if on cue, the door to the inner office opened and he appeared in the doorway.

It was clear from his appearance that he was of Eastern European extraction. "Can I help you?" His appearance was confirmed by his accent which she identified as Romanian.

"Police," said Mandy.

"We do nothing illegal here, "he said defensively. "We merely offer an advertising platform on the web for women, who offer escorting services and companionship. We take the calls from the clients and after making security checks put them in touch with the girls. We take a small fee for the service. Any further service negotiated between the girls and their clients is nothing to do with us."

"Right," said Sam. "Listen sunshine, I know a pimp when I see one so cut the crap. We just want straight answers to straight questions. We are not interested in your sleaze ball operation but we could be if you jerk us around. We are investigating a murder, get it?"

"I get it," said Vasilescu. "Please sit. How can I help?"

"Do you know this Girl?" said Mandy passing the photo of their deceased victim to him.

He studied the photo and looked shocked as it dawned on him that he was looking at a post mortem picture. "She is dead?"

"Murdered, do you recognise her?"

"The girl killed at Church?" he continued. "I did not know…"

"Do you know her?"

"Yes, she was one of the girls that worked here a while back."

"Do you have a name," asked Sam.

"Christine Marstone, I think. Lisa should have her phone number," he indicated to the middle aged woman who had let them in.

"What can you tell us about her?"

"She was with us for a while. The girls come and go. Change their names and appearance and move around from town to town. The clients always look for someone new and fresh."

"And Christine, did she have regulars."

"She hasn't worked through us for a year, perhaps eighteen months. She started her own thing."

"Sex parties?" said Mandy.

"She stopped using us and concentrated on them. She would have three or four regular girls and hold a couple of parties at different locations each week. They would be fifteen to twenty punters at each party, two parties a day. They would pay between eighty and a hundred pounds each to attend."

"We get the picture," said Mandy.

"Going back, did she have any regulars?"

"A few, some blokes always request the same escort."

"Any problem ones, violent and so on or obsessive, you know the type of thing?" followed up Mandy.

"Now you mention it there was one guy who claimed to be in love with her. Wouldn't leave it alone, flowers, chocolates, presents, the usual bollocks, we blocked him in the end. She wouldn't take any more bookings with him in the end."

"Details," said Sam?

"Lisa might have a mobile number, if she kept, it but that's all we would have."

"Well, we have her name confirmed. She is clearly the same girl that sent the flowers to Kelly when she was in hospital," said Mandy as she drove them out of the yard and back towards the Station.

"It is beginning to hang together, Kelly and Christine were both working girls and they knew one another. We know that Christine visited Kelly in hospital, when she overdosed."

"I am guessing for whatever reason Christine needed to make herself scarce and when Kelly's parent's offered to take their daughter back to Bristol with them, she went along. Perhaps she was going to stay with them and support Kelly. Who knows? I am pretty certain she was in the car when it crashed, took Kelly's ID and walked away," she said.

"She can't just have wandered off along the hard shoulder of the M4. She would have been spotted and picked up," said Sam.

"Perhaps the accident investigation and CCTV will give us the answers."

"We still have no motive," he said.

"We can start by looking into Vasilescu. See if he has history. He doesn't look like the kind of bloke that likes the girls to go out on their own. He certainly had motive in sending a message to the other girls not to set up in competition. A pimp is a pimp however you dress it up."

"I have the phone number of her admirer come stalker from that Lisa. We should be able to get an address and real name from the provider and take it from there."

"At least we have some lines of enquiry," said Mandy. "For a while there I thought I was going to bomb on my first case."

"Well failure is always an option," said Sam as they pulled into car park at the Station

Chapter 18

Mandy found herself in the office used by Superintendent Taylor on his visits to Eastbourne. He was in a hurry. Brighton was the venue for a planned massive protest to remain in the European Union and have a second referendum. Three years earlier, the UK had voted to leave but only by a narrow majority. The Parliament was split with the Majority of members in favour of remaining. Defying the result of the referendum, the remainers, as they were known, had used every parliamentary trick in the book to frustrate any attempt to leave. Protests, both in favour of leave or remain were on the increase. Brighton had the only Green Party Member of Parliament in the UK and was overwhelmingly made up of remainers. Eastbourne, with a mostly retired and aging population, was overwhelmingly made up of leavers.

"We have thousands of Remainers marching at the week-end in Brighton and we have a rally being held in Eastbourne by the newly formed Brexit party. We are thinly stretched," said Taylor by way introduction.

"That is unfortunate but I don't have enough officers to follow things up in a timely fashion," said Mandy.

"Reading the files, it looks to me like you are there already."

Mandy knew he wanted a quick result. She also knew that giving him what he wanted might move her career onwards, or alternatively it could go sideways. "I am not convinced," she said.

"The Vicar..." he started to look through the paperwork.

"Reverend Grant," she offered.

"Yes, this Reverend Grant had the opportunity to murder our victim and then he kills himself in a fit of remorse."

"We have no proof of that."

"Do you have any other suspects? No, you don't and it fits."

She realised that Taylor had to be under pressure to get the case solved. Resources were scarce and a dead prostitute was not high on the 'to do list.' She took a deep breath and replied politely. "We are developing leads," she said.

"Not fast enough to justify the resources." He lowered the tone of the conversation, adopting a more placatory approach. "Look, you have done a good job here. Your superiors are impressed. You can wrap it up, notch up a success and move on to bigger and better things. You understand what I am saying here?"

She understood exactly and that was her problem. Don't make waves. Announce the case was solved in record time. All take credit for a job well done and then she would make progress up the greasy pole.

"I am sorry, but I do not accept that. I will continue the investigation," she said resolutely

Taylor masked obvious annoyance. "Very well, carry on Inspector."

She left the office feeling that her future prospects in the Force had taken a knock. "Penny for them," said Sam.

"It's nothing, Taylor thinks it is an open and shut case and the Vicar did it."

"The Vicar, in the car park with the knife," he laughed at his own reference to the game Cluedo.

"Do you think he's right?" she asked.

"You are asking me, my opinion? Now there's a turn up," said Sam. "I thought you new breed of posh coppers had all the answers. Surely you have an app on your Police phone that will run an algorithm that will answer that with a ninety-nine percent probability."

"Well?"

"No, he is talking out his arse and worrying about the budget and his future. That's why he had been promoted to the job. Cuts in budgets lead to cuts in good practice."

"Okay, let's get this done," she said, as she opened the door to the incident room.

The team gathered around the white board and waited. "So what's new team?" said Sam.

Potts could not wait to speak. "We have got into our victim's computer. The IP provider had given us everything we need." The was a pseudo cheer from the rest of the detectives,

"Yes, hooray," he laughed.

"And?" said Mandy.

"She only had one account she accessed on the laptop. She deleted as she went, so there is limited history."

"So after all this effort we are no further forward?"

"No, we are a lot further on. If you remember her fiancé, in his statement, mentioned someone called Jeff, an ex boyfriend or something, who he glimpsed an email from."

"Yes, yes," Mandy was becoming impatient.

"We have emails from him and her replies. I have printed them off." He passed them round.

"My love, we belong together. I know that you feel the same. He cannot control you. You must not be afraid. You must break free and come to me. It is destiny. Jeff.

"Stop it. You understand nothing. There is no us," her reply.

"You are only saying that but I know different. You are just frightened of him. I shall protect you. Be mine."

"Listen you creep. Just fuck off."

"You don't mean that. After all I gave you."

"Fuck off. You were just another punter. Can't you get that through your thick head?"

"You bitch, you will pay for this. You'll see."

"I have edited them down to give you the flavour," said Potts. "I have emailed the full transcripts to you all, but you get the gist of it."

"So I think we have our suspect," said Mandy. "This Jeffrey is obviously an ex client of Christine's when she was on the game with Happy escorts or whatever they were called. It is clear that in his mind that he thinks they have a relationship where none exists. We can speculate that she took advantage of his obsession, had no problem taking his money and then dumping him."

"Potts, get this bloke's IP address and track him down. We also have his mobile number from the escort agency," said Sam.

"We need to look at John Draper, the fiancé again. From the email it looks like he was abusing our victim," said Mandy.

Siskin spoke. "I'll check the hospitals and see if a Christine Marstone has been admitted with suspected domestic violence injuries."

"And for Christ's sake, let's find out what the Vicar was doing in all this. Chase up technical support. They must be into his laptop by now," said Sam.

"Let's get to it," said Mandy.

Chapter 19

"I have the popcorn," said Sam. "Start the movie."

Mandy, he and Constantinou were gathered around the desk looking at the computer screen. "So I have the accident report from Traffic on the crash that killed Kelly Albright and her parents on the M4 motorway. It occurred just about a mile after the Membury Services," Constantinou began.

"Was the crash picked up on the motorway cameras?" said Mandy.

"No, unfortunately not."

"So what do you have for us?" said Sam.

"Well it appears that the Albrights we driving on the inside lane, doing about forty to forty five miles an hour when they were rear-ended by an articulated lorry. It was later found that the driver, who was Hungarian, had been driving without a break for nearly fourteen hours. He is being prosecuted, but it hasn't got to the Courts yet."

"I see, sounds familiar," said Mandy.

"Anyway, the Police crash report only records three people in the car, Kelly and her parents. Kelly and her father were dead at the scene and mum dies a few hours later in hospital. Now, if your theory is correct, Christine Marstone was in the car and on her way to Bristol with her friend."

"So far we have nothing to back that up and this hasn't helped," said Mandy.

"You're right, but I did a bit of thinking. Given that the car was travelling so slowly and the proximity of the Service Area, I wonder if they had not stopped and were in the process of re-joining the motorway."

"So I started checking the CCTV from the services area," said Constantinou. "And here is the first clip."

They watched as Kelly and an elderly couple, presumably her parents, entered the '"Welcome Break. They watched as the three of them got drinks from a vending machine. They stood drinking from the plastic cups by the exit."

"No sign of Christine with them," said Sam.

"Wait," said Constantinou.

Kelly and her parents finished their drinks, Kelly took the empty cups and disappeared out of shot, presumably to put the cups in a rubbish bin. After about a minute she walked back into the picture with Christine Marstone. "See, there's our victim. I think she ran ahead to use the toilet. Kelly with her slower moving elderly parents, followed her in, a few minutes later."

"So we were right," said Mandy." She was in the car when it crashed."

"Exactly twelve minutes and twenty three seconds after this video, I can place them paying for petrol. Mr Albright used his credit card at the service station. Then, just under three minutes later they were involved in the fatal collision as they re-joined the M4."

"So what happened next?" said Sam.

"Well, I can show you," said Constantinou.

She clicked on the next file and the screen showed the inside of a Burger King. "There," said Constantinou, pointing at the laptop, "see?"

"It is definitely her," said Sam.

"Now she sits there for about three hours. She engages with a number of people. She seems to be waiting."

"For the Police to clear the motorway or to be sure that they are not looking for her," said Mandy.

"Who knows, but she moves to the hallway leading to the exit. We lose her on camera for about six minutes. Then I can pick her up leaving with a male."

"Can we see," said Sam.

"Patience, let it load," after a bit of clicking on the keyboard the screen sprang to life. "There she is leaving with a male in his late twenties, early thirties," said Constantinou.

"Pause it," said Mandy. "Can you zoom in?"

They waited while she positioned the cursor over the man's face and started to enlarge and enhance the image. "So far I have been unable to track him down."

"I think we can help you there," said Mandy. "That is her fiancé, John Draper."

"But..?" Constantinou started to speak.

"But he gave us the impression that he had not met her before she came to Eastbourne," said Sam. Constantinou began checking the car registration database. "I have it, he drives a Jaguar F type and I have his registration. "I can check the ANPR and see where his car went, starting at Membury Services."

They waited silently as the database was scanned. "There you go," said Constantinou. "He drove from the service station, M4, M25, M23 then A27 to Eastbourne."

"And straight back to his flat in the Marina," said Sam.

"I think Mr Draper has a few questions to answer, don't you?" said Mandy.

"Boss," Siskin interrupted them. "Can I have a word?"

Mandy and Sam made their way to where he was sitting. "What have you got?" said Sam.

"Hospital records, Christine Marstone, Eastbourne General have a record of her attending. She was beaten up and went to Accident and Emergency."

"When was this? Eighteen days before the accident on the M4," said Sam, looking at the date on the report.

"So that places her in Eastbourne at that time," said Siskin.

"It was a Wednesday," said Sam.

"So?" asked Mandy.

"The last Wednesday of the month, that's when she ran the sex parties in Eastbourne. She and her friends held two parties on that day, the first at eleven a.m. and the second from seven in the evening until about nine o'clock. She turns up badly beaten at A & E about ten forty five. So the party breaks up and she is then beaten up."

"We need to speak to her fiancé. It looks like he knew her well before he claims to have first met her. Who beat her up? Was it him? Did he find out who she really was after they became engaged? Did he find out on the night of the murder. Having found out he was marrying a prostitute, did he decide to kill her and save face with his pious parents?"

"We need to get him in and get a search warrant for his flat."

Chapter 20

Mandy and Sam sat quietly, waiting in the Bishop's office. They had been waiting for over twenty minutes, before the door finally opened and he made his entrance.

"You do realise that I am a very busy man, don't you? I cannot see why you are bothering the Church again. I told you all I knew the last time we met." He said with ill-disguised impatience and a certain amount of disdain.

Sam could not hold his irritation at the pomposity of the man. "I realise that you are very busy, very busy conspiring to cover up for your paedophile fellow clergy. Tell me? Is that what your interpretation of Christ's, 'suffer the little children to come unto me' is?"

The Bishop turned white as what Sam said was absorbed. "I, I," he managed to stammer and bluster at the same time.

Mandy decided to intervene. Sam was angry and the Bishop was defensive. No progress would be possible if matters escalated into a shouting match. "Sit down," she said to him.

The Bishop took his seat behind the ornate desk. "Now my Lord, you need to engage fully and frankly with us. I should say that at this stage you are not under arrest but I am seriously thing of taking you out of here in handcuffs and, who knows, the press might well arrive to take a few pictures."

"I don't understand."

"Oh! I think you do," said Sam.

Mandy looked at her DS, he understood that she was to take the lead in the questioning. He was angry and that was not helping the situation. "We have the results from the forensic examination of the Reverend Grant's computer. We are now in possession of information that suggests that the Reverend Grant may have been part of a paedophile ring. We also have evidenced that the Church, you and other clerics conspired to cover the matter up. I would suggest that you stop withholding information from us and co-operate. Conspiracy to pervert the course of justice and being a party to a crime after the fact are both serious offences and can attract custodial sentences. Now, perhaps you would start by telling us exactly why Grant was moved from Sheffield to Eastbourne."

The Lord Bishop sat looking down at the top of his desk while he contemplated Mandy's statements. "I think I need to consult. I should like to make a phone call before answering any questions."

Sam was not in the mood for procrastination. "You can make your phone call, but then I shall arrest you and then nick the bloke you bell on conspiracy charges. Up to you, we can easily do this at the Nick."

The Bishop looked almost cartoon like as he gulped and turned ashen. "Now," said Mandy, "I repeat. Tell us exactly why Grant was moved from Sheffield to Eastbourne."

In a corner and unclear what evidence Mandy and Sam had in

their possession, he hesitantly began to talk. "You should understand that this is past and we now have,"

"I know the phrase, robust safeguards in place," said Sam. "And I am sick and tired of hearing it. It is words that mean nothing to the kids who these bastards are taking advantage of. Now cut the crap and answer the question."

"There was cause for concern about the Reverend Grant's behaviour going back a number of years but nothing concrete. Then a specific complaint was made by a concerned parishioner. Following discussions with a Church representative, the parents of the Child decided that matters should not be pursued further and no formal charges were laid."

"Were the Police informed?" asked Mandy.

"It was not deemed necessary," said the Bishop.

"It was brushed under the carpet in other words," said Sam.

"Well, I wouldn't say that."

"No, I wouldn't expect you to," Sam followed up.

Mandy raised her hand in the air to bring an end to the heated exchange, "Carry on."

"It was a difficult time for all concerned. The police were under fire for their handling of the grooming scandal in Rotherham, as were Social Services. There was no appetite to escalate matters," he continued.

"And the Verger, Steven Moore?" said Mandy.

"It just all added to the mess. With a massive Asian grooming ring and now the murder of a girl by the Verger of the same Church, matters were dropped against the Reverend Grant and he was moved."

"And what steps were taken to make sure that he was not a danger to other children?" said Sam.

The Bishop began to speak, "We have instigated a number…"

"Not the bloody robust safeguards speech again. Please don't insult our intelligence," said Sam.

"In other words, you just moved him?" said Mandy.

The Bishop remained silent.

"Well let me tell you what your so called robust safeguards produced. We have the forensics back on the Reverend Grant Laptop. It makes sickening reading. He had over three thousand indecent images of children on it. Nearly two thousand of those were category A. Some of them depicting acts of sexual abuse on babies and toddlers. This is what you are covering up and allowing to happen."

"And it would still be happening if not for us taking his computer to check who was at his Alpha Meetings," said Sam. "The Church did nothing, nothing to stop it. You just set about covering your arses."

"If I had my way I would arrest the lot of you up to and including the Arch Bishops," said Mandy.

"But we all know that is not going to happen," said Sam.

Outside, sitting in the car, Sam was calming down. "Look on the bright side, at least he killed himself," said Mandy.

"And we have lost the chance to expose the extent of the cover up taking place within the Churches and institutions across the Country. It makes me sick," he said as he started the engine.

"We pass it on to the specialist child protection unit for them to deal with. We have a murder to investigate," said Mandy.

Chapter 21

"For the purposes of the video disc, would you please state your name," said Mandy.

"John Nicholas Draper,"

"Present at the interview is Detective Inspector Mandy Pile."

"And Detective Sergeant Samuel Shaw," said Sam.

"Please confirm Mr Draper, that you have waived your right to have a solicitor present?"

"I don't need a solicitor. I have done nothing. Why have your arrested me?"

"You have been informed of your right to remain silent and you are aware that you do not have to say anything. But, it may harm your defence if you do not mention, when questioned, something which you later rely on in court. Anything you do say may be given in evidence. This interview is being video taped," said Sam.

"Yes, yes what is this all about?"

They were sat in an interview room at Eastbourne Police

Station. Mandy and Sam had arrested Draper at his place of work. They had previously obtained a warrant to search his flat in Sovereign Harbour. As they spoke, a team was searching his home. They had gained entry using his own keys, taken at the time of his arrest.

We are interviewing you in connection with the murder of Christine Marstone. Did you know that Miss Albright was in reality a young woman known as Christine Marstone?" said Mandy.

"No, of course not," said Draper.

"Are you absolutely certain?"

"I told you already. We were to marry, I have never heard the name Christine Marstone."

Mandy continued, ignoring Draper's increasingly angry denials. "In your earlier statement you said that you first met Christine at a fast food outlet in Eastbourne. Is that correct?"

"I said I met Kelly in Eastbourne." He emphasised the name. "I have never heard of this Christine."

"Just to be clear, the first time you ever met this young woman was here in Eastbourne. You had never had any contact prior to that meeting?"

"I just told you."

"I should like you to have you look at this piece of CCTV footage. It was taken at Membury Services," said Sam, as he passed his laptop across the desk that sat between them.

"Just press any key and it will start to play," said Mandy.

They watched as Draper viewed the CCTV footage of the night that Kelly and her parents were killed and Christine assumed her friend's identity. The colour in Draper's face began to drain as he realised he had been trapped in a lie. The footage stopped and he sat looking down, avoiding Mandy and Sam's gazes. Sam lent across and retrieved the laptop.

"You just told me that you first met Christine in Eastbourne and that you were unaware of her true identity. How then do you explain the CCTV footage I have just shown you?"

"I was just a chance meeting, she wanted a lift."

"What were you doing at the Services?"

"I had been to Bristol and just stopped to use the toilet and get something to eat. I just met her and gave her a lift."

"Are you telling us you just happened to be there? Picked up a random woman, and then took her home with you and then what? She just moved in and stayed?" said Mandy incredulously.

"Yes, that is more or less it," he replied.

"Can you see why we might find that version of events hard to believe," said Sam.

"It is the truth."

"You do realise that through the Automatic Number Plate Recognition System we will be able to track your car on the night in question? So I ask again, did you arrange to meet Christine Moore at the Services? Did she call you and ask you to get her? Did you in fact drive from Eastbourne to do so?"

"No, no, I have already told you, I was driving back from Bristol and met her by chance."

"Were you aware that Christine was engaged in prostitution?"

He looked genuinely shocked. "I don't understand."

"Did you know that she was a prostitute?" said Sam.

"No, I don't believe you."

"Let me put to you what actually happened," said Mandy. "I think you had met Christine previously in Eastbourne. She made monthly visits here with her co-sex workers and ran, effectively, a pop up brothel. She and a couple of girls, worked on a monthly rota in Sittingbourne, Hastings, Brighton, Chelmsford and other towns. They used social media to advertise their, so called, gangbang parties. Have you ever attended such a party, Mr Draper?"

"No, of course not,"

"In any event, I believe at some stage you met Christine, probably as you said at a McDonalds or Kentucky Fried chickenand you became intimately acquainted with her at some stage."

"No," he insisted.

"I think you got a phone call the night of the crash. She probably told you some story about leaving a boyfriend. She had been beaten severely and hospitalised a few weeks prior."

"Unless you were responsible for her injuries?" interrupted Sam.

"I don't understand?"

"Did you beat Christine up, resulting in her attending Eastbourne General Hospital?" said Mandy.

It was clear that, confronted with the CCTV, he was beginning to panic and was becoming increasingly agitated, "No, I keep telling you."

"If we accept that you were unaware that she was a working girl, that would give you clear motive for murder."

"I haven't murdered anyone."

Mandy continued. "I put it to you that, if we accept that it was a chance encounter at the Service Area and you gave her lift to Eastbourne, then the following sequence of events occurred." Mandy paused and studied Draper. He seemed to be confused, ready to break?

She pushed on. "Unaware that your intended was a prostitute, you became engaged, introduced her to your parents and the local Church congregation. You began preparations for the wedding. Then what happened? Did you find out that she was a common whore? Did you realise that you would bring shame on your family and make you all a laughing stock?"

He said nothing, head bowed.

"You found yourself trapped. You decided to kill her."

"I didn't kill her," he shouted.

"So why did you lie about meeting her in Eastbourne?" said Sam.

"You are right. I met her three months before. It was in the Kentucky and things developed from there. I knew her as Kelly. We would meet once a month. She said her work brought her here once a month and she finished at about ten at night. She told me she was in PR, that her client was international. She worked late because of the time zone difference. She came here to oversee their monthly social media campaign."

"In fact she and the other girls were running monthly sex parties here in Eastbourne. One between eleven o'clock and one, to catch the lunch time trade and another between seven and nine in the evening," said Sam.

"So you met after work and she stayed at your flat?" said Mandy.

"Yes, but I swear I knew nothing of the sex parties."

"Go on."

"One night I went to meet as usual and found her covered in blood and in pain. She told me she had been mugged waiting for me to pick her up. I took her to the hospital and she was admitted."

"Did she say who had beaten her up?"

"No, just that she had been mugged. Anyway I went back to the hospital the next evening after work to see how she was. They had no record of her ever being admitted."

Sam looked at Mandy. They knew that Kelly had been admitted under her own name of Christine Marstone. If Draper had been asking for Kelly Albright, they indeed would have no records.

"When did you see her after that?"

"Not until she called me to come to Membury Services."

"So you lied, why?" said Mandy.

"I knew that you would think I killed here."

"Why would that follow," said Mandy.

"I found out on the night she died that she was not who she said she was."

"How did you find out?"

"The Reverend Grant told me."

"How did he say he came by this information?" asked Mandy.

"He wouldn't say. Said that it was a parishioner and couldn't break a confidence."

"What did you do?"

"Nothing, I just thought it a load of nonsense. There is always some pious hypocrite at the congregation that likes to stir things up. It is not the first time. They love a bit of scandal. Then when she was murdered I panicked."

The door opened at that point and a uniformed constable entered and whispered in Mandy's ear."

"One further question, there was no mobile phone found among Christine's personal effects or in the car park where she was murdered. Did you take her phone?" she said.

"I didn't know that. No I didn't."

"Her phone has been found hidden, during the search of your flat. Did you kill her and take the phone in an attempt to cover up her identity?"

"No, I didn't kill her."

"So we won't find your finger prints on it? We won't find information revealing her activities as a prostitute that you may have had access to, information that decided her fate that night?"

"No, no," he was verging on the hysterical.

"I put it to you that on the night of her death you found out she was not who you thought she was. You found the truth from reading her phone messages. Enraged, feeling a fool, a cuckold and betrayed, you decided to murder her. You stabbed her in the Church car park and took her phone to hide the truth?"

Chapter 22

"Okay, let's get the troops together. Bail Draper, pending further enquiries," said Mandy as Sam entered her office. He left to organise Drapers release and get the team to the incident room.

She sat and stared at the top of her desk. She was under pressure to get matters cleared up. Matters were not getting any clearer though. She knew that Taylor was being pushed to release resources. She couldn't blame him for the cuts and to an extent, he was also a victim of them. He was doing a Chief Superintendent's job in all but pay. She knew she needed to put that out of her mind, she was determined to solve this murder and get it right.

She thought about Draper's evidence. On the face of it, it seemed to hang together. He could have meet Christine earlier and lied to the Police when confronted with her murder. She could well have concealed that she was a prostitute. When he found out though, he could well have murdered her in a fit of rage at being made a fool of.

Somebody knew her true identity in the Alpha Church Group and made Draper aware of it. The question was, of course, who? The Vicar might have been told it by someone and passed it on to Draper, or he himself could have found it out and decided to tell him.

She could not rule the Reverend Grant out. Christine inhabited the shady world of porn and prostitution. She could have learnt of the Vicars abuse of children. She might well have been blackmailing him. He could have had a motive to want her dead. He had committed suicide and they had assumed it was to do with the child porn on his computer. Did he really think that the Police would examine his laptop in any detail, when all they wanted was a list of who attended the Alpha meetings over the past few weeks? Perhaps he realised, having murdered Christine, it was only a matter of time. Seeing no way out, he had killed himself.

Then there was Matthew Shelley, the overly pious parishioner and the verger Steven Moore who was a convicted murderer. Was there a link? She realised the more they knew, the less matters were clearing.

Her thoughts were interrupted. "They are waiting for you," said Sam. Giving a deep sigh, she left her office and went to get a progress update.

"Tell me, what do we have?"

Potts spoke first. "We have an address for the stalker who was threatening our victim. We have tracked the IP address and from that, the location."

"Finally," said Sam.

"Okay, we need to interview him," said Mandy. "What else do we have?"

Siskin spoke. "Christine's phone, we have all the text messages and contacts," he held aloft a pile of paper.

"Get on that. We need to track everyone she had contact with."

"There's more," he said.

"Go on."

"They found the phone hidden in Draper's and her flat. It was in the kitchen. You know the cornice that runs around the top of kitchen cabinets. It was tucked behind it, on top of one of the cupboards, simple but effective."

"Fingerprints?" said Mandy.

"Only our victims," he replied.

"So the assumption is that she concealed it there herself. She did not have it with her when she went to the Church. If Draper had killed her, then his prints would be on it. There is no indication that he was wondering around the Church wearing gloves. If he had killed her, taken it and then wiped it, then her prints would have been removed as well."

"We are having it checked for DNA. That will take a lot more time," said Siskin.

"As you know, Sam and I ..."

"I have one more thing to add," interrupted Siskin.

"Sorry, carry on," said Mandy.

"There was a tracker app on her phone. Someone was keeping tabs on her."

"That is interesting. We need to know who. Check all the phones of the suspects and let's see if we can't find out who it was. Start with Draper."

"Now as I was saying, Sam and I interviewed Draper earlier. He admits to lying as to when he first met Christine but that doesn't make him the murderer. I have to admit though, he had motive and opportunity. On reflecting on the interview, there was one thing that didn't hang together. He consistently denied knowing her true identity"

"So what's the problem?" said Sam.

"The timing," she replied. "If he met Christine earlier, why would she call herself Kelly Albright? We assumed she took the identity when she and her parents were killed in a car crash, but months before, Draper said she told him that her name was Kelly Albright."

Merryweather spoke. "It may not be too much of a mystery. Look, he met her after she had been holding a gangbang sex party."

"Yes so?"

"The adverts for the parties show the same girls wearing different clothing, wigs and even masks. There were just three of four girls at each party, the same three of four. To keep it fresh and the punters interested they dressed differently and changed their names. It gave the appearance that there were new girls every month. A girl would be blonde Mandy one month, Red haired Scarlet the next, or Kelly and so on."

"So you think she just gave the name she was using that day - Kelly," said Sam.

"Then word association took over and when Draper got to know better and wanted to know more, she said the first surname that came into her head, her friend's Albright."

"It's possible," admitted Mandy. "That leaves, who beat her up resulting in her ending up in A&E. If we believe Draper, he didn't see her after that until he got the call to go and pick her up at the Service Area, the night the Albright's died in a car crash and she took her new identity and resumed her relationship with Draper."

"We need to know who beat her up and who she was in hiding from."

Chapter 23

It was mid-afternoon when Mandy and Sam left the Station at Southgate in north London. They made their way outside. "There it is," said Sam.

The blue and white police car was parked in the road behind McDonalds as arranged. Mandy was met by one of the two uniformed officers who stepped out from the passenger side as they approached.

"DI Pile," he addressed Sam. Sam pointed to Mandy.

"Pleased to meet you," she said. "Thank you for acting as a taxi."

"No problem, we have to go anyway. We are meeting the family liaison team there."

"He has not been told yet?" asked Sam.

"No, there are a lot of victims these days and we are stretched. Knife crime is out of hand, senseless but no stopping it," he said resignedly, as he got back in the passenger seat and Sam and Mandy got in the rear.

As they sat in the traffic, Mandy took the time to re-read the file. Once they had Christine Marstone's name, they had done a search for relatives. She had a sister who appeared to have moved to New Zealand that they had been unable to trace. Her mother had abandoned the family when the girls were still at school. They had tracked her down, but she had died some seven years earlier. Her remaining closest relative was her father, who lived in council accommodation in Edmonton, North London.

She read his record. After his wife left, he seemed to turn to drink, or at least increased his consumption. He had a record of arrests, mostly drink related public order offences. The record painted a picture of a chaotic life. Christine and her sister Cheryl had been fostered and taken into care on and off, as their father's drink problem increased or abated.

The girls, it was clear to her, had little chance in the real World. Both had run away from care as soon as they had an opportunity. Mandy was beginning to get an understanding of the victim. Starting by being abandoned by her Mother, brought up by an alcoholic father in deprived and poverty stricken circumstances, it was hardly surprising that she had gravitated into sex work.

It was a familiar story, working as an escort or prostitute greatly increased the chances of being the victim of violent crime. Christine had, on the face of it, escaped from that life style. She was working, had a fiancé and was getting married. It would seem though that her past had not given up on her and Mandy knew that the key to her death lay somewhere in her history.

The police car eventually pulled up on the Council Estate by a block of flats. "We shall wait here. The victim support officer is already on site," said the officer driving.

"There's no need. We can get a cab to a station," said Sam.

"Probably best if we wait. This is not the best place to be a copper, especially female or old."

They made their way to Mr Marstone's flat. "That was sexist," said Mandy.

"Fuck sexist," said Sam. "What did he mean old, cheek?"

He mumbled on a bit more about young coppers, respect and what it was like in the olden days until they reached the flat that they had been looking for. "This seems to be it," said Mandy.

The door was open and voices could be heard from inside. It was clear that her father had just been informed of her death. They caught the tail end of a conversation. A policewoman was saying "two detectives should be here any minute and they should be able to answer some of your questions Mr Marstone."

The flat smelt and clearly was uncared for. Mr Moore had obviously no interest in how he lived. There was filth and clutter everywhere, peeling wallpaper and paint and a glimpse, through the open door of the bathroom revealed it to be black with mould and with a toilet filled with excrement.

"What a shit hole," commented Sam.

Mandy gave him a reproachful look before pushing open the door to the living room from where the voices emanated. Inside Mr Moor sat on a filthy sofa with numerous cigarette burns on it. He was in soiled jeans and wore a crumpled stained T-shirt, that also had evidence of cigarette burns down the front. Overflowing ash trays, empty bottles and beer cans littered the floor. The curtains had only been partially drawn open, leaving the room in semi darkness. Mandy had to admit that Sam's description was accurate. It was a shit hole and

Mr Moore was clearly a man who had given up.

She noted the female support officer had remained standing. She determined to do the same. The available seating was filthy. "My name is Mandy Pile and this is Sam Shaw. We are investigating your daughter's murder."

The officer made herself known as Jackie Hetherington. Greetings were exchanged and Mandy continued. "I am sorry for your loss, Mr Marstone. I assure you we will do our utmost to catch her killer."

He looked up at Mandy. His eyes watery and bloodshot pleaded with her. It was clear that despite his obvious failings as a father he held genuine feelings for his daughter. "Just get the bastard for me. She didn't deserve this. She was a sweet child."

Sam had taken his note book and pencil from his pocket and waited for Mandy to start the interview. It would be difficult. Drink was hardly an aid to clarity of thought. "I need you to tell me as much as you can about your daughter and her life."

"She was a good girl," he rambled.

"She was. Have you had much contact over the years?"

"She left when she was old enough. I did my best after her mum left."

"I am sure you did. Where did she go when she left home?"

"Here and there, up west, usual. She was a dancer. She liked dancing at school. She had ballet lessons when she was little before her mum went. She liked dancing."

"Do you know where?"

"Usual clubs and pubs, she danced in America too. Did you know that, Las Vegas? That's where all the top stars go."

It was a struggle to keep his thoughts on track and get him to focus. Years of alcohol abuse had dimmed his thinking. Mandy persevered in the hope of getting something of use. "When did she go to Las Vegas?"

"Some years ago, I saw her when she came back. She came to visit me. They gave me money, her and her friend."

"Who was her friend, a girlfriend?" asked Mandy.

"No, a bloke, one of those Eastern Europeans, Hungarian, Pole something like that, she had met him in Las Vegas, she said."

"Do you remember his name?"

"Jimmy, Sunny, Bobby, yes that was it."

"What was it?" said Sam.

"I just told you, Bobby, something foreign or other."

"Do you know how or where they met? Did they meet here or America."

He seemed to be confused and sat thinking for a while. "There, they met in America. I remember she showed me pictures on her mobile of them in Las Vegas and other places over there. They met there and then they came here."

Suddenly he became agitated. "I want you all to fuck off now."

The three police were obviously keeping him from the drink. He hauled himself to his feet and made to the kitchen or what had once been a kitchen but now was a greasy, filth stained wreck of a space. He was unsteady and staggered across the room. "Fuck off he repeated, as he located a two litre bottle of cheap cider among the rubble of the kitchen.

It was self-evident that there was little more to be obtained in the form of useful information from Mr Marstone. "We'll leave you to it then Jackie," said Sam as they made their way to the door.

"Right," replied PC Jacqueline Hetherington. "If he tells me anything useful I shall pass it on." Mandy and Sam left her to it and were relived to breathe, even the polluted London air outside the flat.

Chapter 24

Mandy walked over to Sam's desk carrying two coffees. "For me?" he feigned surprise, "such generosity!"

"I feel it is important to show that I am not above the menial tasks that the lowlier of you have to undertake on a daily basis. As you know, my servants and minions generally cater to my every whim but in the spirit of friendship I have demeaned myself on this occasion by buying a cup of coffee for you my lackey."

"Well, whatever you motives, I am pleased to accept your gift," he replied.

"I am not that posh. Am I?"

"Well …" there was a long pause as Sam considered his reply.

"Come on, I shall not be offended."

"Yes," said Sam.

"Is that it?"

"Yes, you are that posh," he said.

"Right, I see."

"Don't feel bad about it. It is not your fault that your Dad was rich, you went to a private school and then on to Oxbridge and you speak with a plumy accent," he smiled. "It could have happened to anyone of us. You were just unlucky, that is all. You shouldn't let it hold you back in life"

She laughed. "That's pretty much how it was. I still feel I am a good copper though?"

"I think you have all the makings but..."

"But?" she asked.

"Communication, most of the people we deal with and admittedly a lot of them are low life, react negatively to authority. A posh accent plays into their preconceptions and they automatically become un-cooperative. You need to find a way of overcoming their prejudices and connect. There is an innate dislike of the posh among the criminal classes. After all, the only time they usually come into contact with an Oxford accent is when the Judge is banging them up for a few years."

"I'll try and sound less like a Judge handing out a sentence. I will conduct the interview and try and sound more, more..."

"Human," suggested Sam.

Mandy glared at him, "have you finished your coffee? Let's get on with the interview," she said, as she turned and left in the direction of the interview rooms. Sam gulped down the last of his drink and followed her out.

"Thank you for coming in Mr Shelley. We should just like to go over the details of the night of the murder," said Mandy.

Matthew Shelley was dressed in a blue blazer and slacks. He looked the part of the respectable, Church going, middle aged man. She suspected that he gained pleasure by pointing out other's weaknesses and failings. He was a prude and holier than thou to boot.

"I am pleased to help."

"Perhaps you could start from earlier on in the evening. You were overheard having a discussion with the Vicar, Reverend Grant. Is that so?"

"We were just having a chat while the group arrived for the Alpha course."

"You were actually discussing the victim known to you as Kelly Albright, were you not?"

"Well, yes,"

"Pease tell us what was said?"

He looked slightly abashed. Like most gossip mongers and internet trolls, he liked to do his character assassination with anonymity and from a safe distance. Sitting in the Police station and being exposed to the spotlight was not to his taste. "It was nothing really. I just made an innocuous comment that perhaps her choice of attire was not wholly appropriate for Church. That's all."

Mandy looked at him. She said nothing but continued to stare until she sensed his discomfort. "It was more than that, wasn't it?"

"Well, I may have made certain allusions," he said.

"You called her a prostitute, did you not?"

"Not in those words,"

"In what words then," Mandy persisted?

"Well I suppose you could convey it like that, but it was not my intention to imply anything."

"My question is relatively simple. What was the basis for your statements made to the Vicar about the victim?"

"I was just talking about the way she chooses to dress."

"How was that Mr Shelley?"

"Like a tart, she was always flaunting it," he replied.

"And what, you did not like it? Or did it perhaps arouse and excite you?"

"Of course not,"

"Perhaps you thought she was giving you the come on?"

"I didn't think any such thing."

"Did you follow her into the car park and try it on. Did she laugh at you or mock you. Did you get angry and..."

"That's not true," he was beginning to perspire. I, I... Do I need a lawyer?"

"Do you? Have you something to hide?" Mandy pressed on.

"No I don't. I did nothing."

Mandy switched the tone and in a calmer voice asked. "Did you know the victim before she attended the Alpha meeting? Had you perhaps, seen her around Eastbourne?"

"No, the first time I saw her and her fiancé was at the Church."

"So you never met her before?"

"I just told you that."

"So you had no basis, no knowledge when you called her a whore to the Vicar?"

"It was just a phrase. She dressed like a tart and I thought it inappropriate."

"Thank you, I think that is all I have to ask. Sam do you have anything further for Mr Shelly?"

Sam spoke and Mandy pulled a cell phone from her bag. "Thank you for your time Mr Shelley if we…."

Sam was interrupted by Matthew Shelley's phone ringing in his blazer pocket. "Sorry I forgot turn it off," he said.

"No problem, please answer it," said Sam.

He took the phone from his pocket and put it to his ear, "hello."

"Hello," said Mandy into the cell phone she was holding.

Matthew Shelley looked bewildered. "You just phoned me?"

"Actually this is the victim's phone. We found it at the flat she shared with her fiancée. It has the numbers of, for want of a better word, her clients on it."

Shelly's mouth gaped open and he his face turned ashen.

"I ask you again, did you know the victim and had you previously availed yourself of her services?"

Chapter 25

It was five thirty a.m. Mandy and Sam sat waiting in car in a street in Brighton. The sun was just rising and casting an orange glow over the sea. "I don't usually see the Sun come up," said Mandy.

"Not unless you have been out all night partying," mumbled Sam.

"You don't like young people, do you Sam?"

"I have nothing against them apart from the fact that they are young and have more fun than me," he joked.

"Anyway, my partying days are long behind me at Uni," she replied.

The radio and Sam responded. "All units are in place."

"Let's hope we have the right address or someone is going to have the worst alarm call ever," she said.

"No need to worry. They are sure that they have tracked the IP of Christine's stalker here. The uniformed boys have done background checks. There are thee flats in the block. Two have single mums and their children in. There is one occupied by a single male named Jeffrey

Abbot and that is the one we are hitting. It is not the name we got from our visit to Vasilescu at the escort agency that Christine worked for, but the cell phone tracks to this location."

"Makes sense," agreed Mandy. "He is our best lead as a suspect. He sent her threatening emails and seemed to be convinced they had a relationship in his head. She probably hardly remembered who he was, just another punter to her, I should guess."

"Anyway we have warrants for the other two flats just in case, but my money is on this Abbot," he said.

There was another voice on the radio and Sam spoke again. "They are all in place and ready to go."

"Give the order," she said.

Two police vans rushed into the street and police jumped out and ran towards the block of flats. The flats were in a converted terraced house. Mandy and Sam watched as a queue of police lined up at the front door. The finally got through the front door and rushed in and up the stairs, to the top floor flat where Jeffrey Abbot lived.

The officers were making a lot of noise, Mandy watched as lights came on in bedrooms up and down the street. The noise was intentional. It spread confusion and disorientation among the suspects in the building and allowed the Police to establish control.

Mandy went to exit the car. "Let things quieten down first," advised Sam.

They sat and waited. Sam's radio came to life. He listened for a moment and turned to Mandy. "I think we need to go in now."

They made their way across the street and watched as the

majority of the raiding party left and drove off. The Policeman on the entrance let them pass as they made their way up the stairs. The passageway was grubby and had not seen a coat of paint in years. The door to Abbot's flat lay smashed and was guarded by another uniformed officer. He spoke, "you need to cover your feet."

Puzzled, Mandy and Sam put the stretch plastic shoe protectors, he handed them over their shoes. They would prevent anyone walking material into a crime scene and contaminating it.

"What is that dreadful smell?" said Mandy.

"It's a smell you will get used to in this job, trust me," said Sam as they walked down the corridor to the room at the end where an uniformed sergeant stood in the doorway.

He stepped aside to allow them to look in. "I have called the forensic service and they will be here soon."

Mandy retched as they entered. The smell was nauseatingly pungent and sickly at the same time. Lying in the middle of the room was a body of a male in his mid-thirties. Decomposition had started and the stomach was bloated with gas given off by the decaying flesh.

Mandy fought down the urge to vomit. "If you are going to be sick it would be better if you didn't contaminate the crime scene," said the uniform.

Controlling the heaving in her stomach, she managed to answer. "I am okay."

Sam, during the course of his career had seen more than enough dead bodies and carried on into the room. "Looks like suicide, he hung himself."

"We cut him down. We had to double check he was dead," said the Sergeant. "We were pretty certain he was by looking at him but you have to be sure."

"Looks like he's not been dead that long," said Sam, "a few days?."

"Oh yeah, he is only just on the turn, so definitely days. There was no sign of rigor, so he was hanging around for at least a couple of days."

Mandy, recovering her composure spoke. "He hung himself?"

"Looks like it, bit of a palaver though. He used the cable from the TV and tied it round his neck and put it over the hook on the door to the kitchen, more self-strangulation than hanging."

"I have seen that before though," said Sam.

"Mostly sex games gone wrong in my experience, or sadly kids who are depressed and self harming," said the Sergeant.

"Are we sure it was suicide?" said Mandy.

"There was no note."

"We shall have to wait on the forensics now. We shall have a look round, but then there is little to do until they have finished up"

The flat was not large. They had passed by the bedroom and bathroom doors on their way to entering the living room, where the body was found hanging from the door to a small kitchen. They retraced their steps to the bedroom.

"Oh my God," exclaimed Sam as he entered. "Look at this."

"Mandy's eyes adjusted to the darkness as the curtains were still closed. It took her a while to take in what she was seeing. Every inch of wall space was covered in pictures, printed on A4 computer photo paper.

"They are all, of our victim, Christine Marstone," she gasped.

It was a surreal sight. There were pictures on the walls, the back of the door and the ceiling. The room was wallpapered with them. Some of her face, full body and then some just of her hand, her feet in sandals or her hair, every inch of her was enlarged and displayed.

"I think we may have our killer," said Sam.

Chapter 26

"We have had quite a few developments over the past twenty four hours and we all need to be up to speed on recent developments." Mandy was addressing the team in the incident room.

"As you all know, we tracked down our victim's stalker, Jeffrey Abbott to a flat in Brighton. When we gained access we found his partly decomposed body handing from a hook on the back of the kitchen door. DI Pile and I did a quick inspection of the scene before handing over to forensics. Constantinou what have you got for us?" said Sam.

"Search of the body and premises," she answered. "Mr Abbot was clearly obsessed with Christine Marstone and had been stalking her for some time. Apart from the photos of her plastered all over the flat, there were a few notable finds. Firstly, a knife was found that did not match the others. It is about four inches and could have been used to inflict the injuries on the victim."

"Any blood, finger prints or DNA," asked Merryweather.

"No, and that is what makes it significant. It has absolutely nothing on it. Now, a kitchen knife will always have something on it, remains of food, the users DNA or just dirt. This one has been bleached and wiped clean. Given the state of the rest of his flat, Mr Abbot and cleaning products are not well acquainted," said Constantinou.

"Could have been cleaned and planted at the scene," said Mandy, "Anything else?" Constantinou checked the report she held, "A Rolex watch. Now given our victim was on benefits, the watch he was wearing immediately drew the attention of forensics. It was obviously, initially thought to be a cheap knock-off. To everyone's surprise, it is genuine, not only genuine but very high end, worth over two hundred grand new."

"The owner should be easy to locate," said Siskin.

"We are on it," said Potts.

"They also found a hoody with blood on it, same group as our victims and a second spot of blood of a different grouping," said Constantinou. "They are prioritising the DNA analysis."

"The evidence seems to be building against our Jeffery Abbot," said Mandy. "Did they analyse his mobile phone?"

Potts responded. "He was definitely stalking and threatening our victim and has been for a very long time."

"Did he have the tracker app on it?" said Sam.

"No, there was no sign of anything like that. They have tracked the movement of the phone on the night of Christine's murder."

"And," said Mandy?

"His phone did not move from the flat."

"Doesn't prove much really," said Sam. "Anyone who watches a TV crime show knows we can track a mobile phones movements and location. If you were off to commit murder you would just leave your phone at home."

"We do know though that Abbot was not tracking our victim. So how would he know she was at the Church?"

"It was a weekly meeting. The killer knew her routine, possibly," said Mandy.

"Okay, the preliminary report by the Coroner," said Siskin. "Abbot died hours after the murder of Christine Marstone."

"So," said Sam. "He waits for her by the Church, probably knew her routine having stalked her previously. He knows she is in the habit of nipping out the meeting for a quick fag. He sees his chance. He stabs her. He goes back to his flat, bleaches and cleans the knife. He is then filled with remorse having realised that he has killed the love of his life. In a fit of jealousy he tops himself. It works for me."

"Just one small flaw," said Siskin. "The coroner cannot be one hundred per cent sure he committed suicide. There are some marks around his neck tharare not consistent with the ligature used. They used some sort of photographic techniques that brings out latent marks or bruising. There is a hint of a thumb print near the larynx. In other words he could have been strangled and then strung up by the neck."

"But it is not conclusive?" said Mandy.

"There is circumstantial. They found traces of Ketamine in the flat and in his urine in the bladder. He was a known drug user and his record shows he was done for possession of it on two occasions," said Siskin.

"Anybody see anything around the time of the murder?"

Merryweather spoke. "Uniform carried out door to door. "Nobody saw anything unusual. The girl who occupies the ground floor flat said she thought Abbot had a visitor that night but can't be sure. They got the impression she knew he used Ketamine and knew that the dealer delivered. So she paid little attention to it."

"Moving aside from Jeffery Abbot and back to our victim, we need to know much more about her background. Now when we spoke to her father, he said she had been in America and had returned with someone, probably Eastern European. Have we got any further filling in the gaps?" asked Mandy.

"I am coordinating it and we are all trying to pin it down. We know from the US immigration when she entered. She flew from Heathrow direct to Las Vegas. She had a normal tourist visa, valid for six months. She was caught acting as an escort and working illegally in a club, her visa was revoked and she was returned to the UK," said Siskin.

"Was a man returned with her?"

"No mention of it."

"Okay, we need to find out exactly what she did there and with whom," said Mandy. "Stick with it."

"I can think of one eastern European," said Sam.

"So can I, our local pimp, Mr Vasilescu," said Mandy.

"We need to have another chat with him."

"Okay, let's get on the following. CCTV, the night of the murder needs to be examined again. Now we know what Jeffery Abbot looks like let's see if we can place him at the scene. There was blood on his hoody, so chances are he was wearing it and it has a pretty distinctive design, so that should help. Next, chase the lab for the DNA results. We need to know who he came into contact with. Find the owner of the Rolex and how it came to be in his possession. Anything else?" said Mandy.

"A bit of information from Sheffield, apparently one of the detectives who dealt with the murder committed by Steven Moore decided to follow up on the information we got from him in prison. He examined the burials around that time and identified two graves that were dug. He obtained and exhumation order and found the body of a young woman under the coffin. She was a runaway from a children's home in Manchester," said Merryweather.

"Not the result anyone would have wanted, but at least she will now have a proper funeral," said Mandy.

"The World is a shit place sometimes," said Sam.

Chapter 27

They decided to visit Vasilescu's Escort agency in the evening. It was just past ten when Mandy and Sam pulled up in the car park of the industrial unit. The lights were all blazing from the unit he occupied.

"They clearly are very busy in the evenings," said Sam as he got out of the car.

"Yes, it certainly is a hive of activity compared to the last time we dropped in on them."

The outer office, that had only one girl answering phones the last time they called, was now packed with four women and as they looked into Vasilescu's office space they saw that two more were manning phones there as well.

Lisa recognised them from their last visit and called through to Vasilescu. "Them bleeding coppers are back."

"And good evening to you to," said Sam. They walked through to his now crowded office. He had been on a call but quickly severed the connection as they entered.

He sat looking at them for a moment. "We are doing nothing

illegal," he said.

"We got that message the last time we called," said Mandy. "If we were interested, we would have had you raided already. We could still do it, so it would be best if you cooperated fully. Don't you agree?"

"You have my full attention. I am all ears."

"We just need a bit more information about Christine," said Mandy.

Sam took the lead in the questioning. "We spoke to her father. He told us she had been to Las Vegas and outstayed her welcome. He also said that she had returned with some sort of eastern European."

He smiled. "There are a lot of eastern Europeans in the World."

"That is very true. They are not all, of course, known to Christine Marstone though," interrupted Mandy.

"I am not hiding anything. There is no point. I am sure even if it takes you a while, you will be able to track my movements in and out of the UK and you would place me on the same flight as her returning from America."

"So save us the time and effort and tell us all about it," said Sam.

"I had a chance to do a favour for a friend and it involved a free trip to the US of A. So having done the bit of business, I thought I would see what opportunities there were. I was working in Las Vegas when I came across her."

"What sort of work would that be?"

"You know this and that. I would rather avoid details. Anyway she was down on her luck and I admit my plans were not working out."

"Don't tell me, the local pimps were none too keen on foreign competition?"

"Something like that, in any event we struck up a relationship and helped each other out..."

"You acted as her pimp," said Sam.

"Protector," he corrected him.

"Okay, so what happened?"

"Things were going fine for a while and then she came to the attention of the police. You can't do anything in Las Vegas without the backing of the police or the organised crime groups that run the place. The Mob just needed a piece of the action and they, more or less, left you alone. The Police presumably get their share. All is sweet as long as you don't fuck the tourist trade," he said.

"And you brought yourself to their attention?" said Mandy.

"Not on purpose, Christine had a booking at the Venetian Hotel. You know the one with the fake Gondolas inside and done out like Venice. We usually steered clear of the big hotels, the trade there was mob only and it is not a good idea to tread on the wrong toes."

"So you and Christine overstepped the mark and went into the big league?"

"It was too good to pass up. I always stayed close to her and she had her phone on speed dial. If I got a ring I knew that she was in trouble and I needed to act."

"So she was with a punter in the Venetian and things went amiss?" said Mandy.

"Skipping the details, I had to earn my money for once and a couple of rich sleaze balls got hurt. Hotel security got involved and then the Police."

Sam smiled, "Your concept of who is and who isn't a sleaze ball is fascinating. Have you looked in the mirror recently?"

"Go on," said Mandy.

"As I said, the Police got involved. Turned out Christine had overstayed her visa. They did not bring any charges, as the punters, despite the battering I gave them, did not want any publicity. She was returned to the UK and it was suggested that I might like to leave the USA as well. They cancelled my visa and I flew back voluntarily."

"Nice and tidy," said Sam.

"It also explains why you weren't immediately flagged up on the system as no formal charges were brought."

"When you got back?"

"I started this totally legal Escort business and she worked for me."

"But she expanded into running her own sex parties. How did you feel about that?" said Mandy.

"You asked me this the last time. I told you I was fine about it?"

"Well, it's just that we have learned that she was taken into hospital having been beaten up. Do you know anything about that?"

"Of course not, what sort of man do you think I am?"

"A violent sleaze ball who lives off of women, to put it in your own words Mr Vasilescu."

Chapter 28

"There he is at the station," said Merryweather,

"And this is the night of the murder," asked Mandy? She and Sam were watching the CCTV footage from the cameras at Eastbourne Train station, that Merryweather had spent hours reviewing.

"Yes, he is definitely wearing the hoody that was found at Jeffery Abbot's flat or an identical one."

"You can't see his face though," said Sam.

"Well that is probably why he wore a hoody," said Merryweather.

"Don't be facile. I am aware of that, but from an evidential point of view it is not proof that it was him."

"Nevertheless we can assume that he was in Eastbourne around the time Christine Marlstone was murdered," said Merryweather. "He got off the train that arrived from Brighton."

"Okay the time line fits. He arrives in Eastbourne just before eight and he has plenty of time to walk to the Church, were he kills her in the car park. Do we have any footage of him making his way there?"

said Mandy.

"Not very good quality," he jumped to two further clips, one from a camera at a Public House and the other from a convenience store.

"I see what you mean. It is hard to be one hundred percent but it is good enough to say that someone dressed in, more or less, the same way made their way from the train station to the Church. How about after the murder, do we have footage of him leaving Eastbourne?"

"Nothing, it is not conclusive but no one even similar is picked up en route or at the station,"

"He vanished?" said Sam.

"Not vanished, it just seems he did not go back to Brighton by train on the night of the murder."

"Is there any way he could avoid the CCTV at the station?" said Mandy.

"No, all the cameras are working. I have checked and double checked, there is no way that he left by train or the next morning for that matter. We have looked at CCTV up to lunch time the next day."

"So our hoody man travels to Eastbourne from Brighton to Eastbourne by train, murders our victim and vanishes," said Sam.

"We are left with two possibilities, he stayed the night here at a friends or a hotel."

"You can rule that out, we know he returned to Brighton as he committed suicide at his flat."

"So he must have travelled back some other way," said Mandy.

"We are ahead of you there. We checked the bus cameras. He did not board a bus to Brighton."

"Taxi?" said Sam.

"We phoned every company, no single males from Eastbourne to Brighton. It is an expensive trip and there were only two journeys made and both were a group of four sharing."

"That is not possible. Jeffrey Abbot comes here from Brighton by train, commits murder then vanishes only to turn up back at his flat in time to hang himself," said Sam.

Mandy was silent, deep in thought. "There is another explanation."

"Well I would like to hear it?" said Merryweather.

"I need to check a few things first," she said.

Siskin approached them. "The Super's looking for you. He just arrived."

Mandy left them debating as she made her way to see Super Intendent Taylor.

"Congratulations on you promotion Sir," said Mandy as she sat.

"Thank you but these cut backs delay everything. We are all working above our pay grades to keep the budget down," said the now Chief Super Intendent Taylor. "They want us to do more with less."

It was not the reaction Mandy expected, "I assume that was to pre-empt me asking for more resources for my investigation?"

"Sorry, it wasn't targeted at you. It was more a general moan about the shortage of money and police. I am pleased at my promotion, obviously, but there are many good officers that are being kept on lower pay grades to balance the budget. It really is not great for moral."

"So my pay rise is not what the meeting is about, I am guessing."

He laughed. Sadly no, so where are we at?"

"Well, the emphasis of the investigation has now switched to Jeffrey Abbot. It is clear that he was obsessed with the victim, was stalking her and in his mind was in a relationship with her. To her he was nothing more than another punter who had paid for her time."

"It would not be the first time stalkers go on to kill the person they claim to be the love of their lives in a fit jealously for a perceived rejection."

"There is no doubt that Mr Abbot had all the expected traits. He had a history of mental illness, a diagnosis of borderline personality disorder, obsessive, drug use and the usual criminal record that goes with it. His flat was a shrine to the victim. He does fit the profile."

"I understand you can place him in Eastbourne at the time of the murder?"

"Yes, there is CCTV, but it is not good enough to get a positive ID."

"So he had the motive, the means and he was at the scene. So?"

"So I am not convinced he did it," she replied.

"That's not a reason to not finalise matters. Look, you have done amazingly well on your first murder case. You should be congratulating yourself and looking at the prospect of promotion. You have solved a murder of a young woman in Sheffield and even exposed a child abusing vicar as a byproduct of catching the murderer of Christine Marstone. It's the perfect start. Why jeopardise all that. You need to consider your position carefully"

There was a tense silence as Mandy contemplated the situation. She realised that the pressure was on. "I am not happy, Sir. There are still outstanding lines of enquiry. There is Matthew Shelley for one. He was a client. She was in a position to expose him. He had motive."

"You have no real evidence of his involvement."

"He had motive and opportunity. There is also her ex-pimp, Bobby Vasilescu. He was angry that she had started out on her own. He is quite capable of violence and possibly murder. Of that, I have no doubt."

"But no evidence," he repeated.

She realised that the sensible thing to do was close the case and accept Abbot as the culprit. It was that she just did not want to.

There was a knock on the door. Constantinou entered. "Yes?" said Taylor.

"You need to see this," she said handing a piece of paper to Mandy. She read.

"What is it?" he said.

"Full autopsy report, Jeffery Abbot was murdered. It was not suicide."

Chapter 29

"We seem to be going nowhere fast," said Sam as he sat in Mandy's office. He had picked up coffee and sandwiches for lunch for them at the local convenience store. Taylor had returned to Brighton somewhat disappointed that he had been unable to wind up the investigation.

"What is this sandwich supposed to be?" asked Mandy.

"Avocado and something unpronounceable, that is supposed to be a super food from the Andes or somewhere. It is really healthy."

"Right and what is in yours?"

"Bacon, sausage, egg and brown sauce," he took another bite.

"Is it nice?"

"Very, thank you," he said.

"Mine tastes like soggy cardboard and grit."

"The girl in the shop assured me it was on trend. I knew that you only go for the best. It cost fifty pence more than your run of the mill pleb fodder."

"It was a nice thought, but just because you think I am gentry in future, would you mind awfully just sticking to the staple food for coppers. You know, bacon butties, fish and chips and the odd grease burger?"

"If you say so boss," he said wiping a dribble of brown sauce from his chin. Mandy abandoned the sandwich and turned her attention back to the file on her desk "At least Taylor has had to concede more time is needed now."

"It is not really his fault. He is a good copper but we all have to go with the times. The pressure comes all the way down from the top. Time is money and the force is short of money."

"I know, but everyone on the team is working flat out chasing down the lines of enquiries. It gives you no time to sit back, think and get an overview, the bigger picture."

"Is there a bigger picture?"

"We had a theory which seemed reasonable. An ex-prostitute is putting her past life behind her. She adopts a different identity and meets a guy she wants to settle down with. Okay, stealing the identity of a friend killed in a car crash was not the smartest move, but getting a National Insurance number so you can work is not easy. The option was there so she took it."

"So she starts over and then she finds her past life is gradually catching up with her."

"Yes, first she runs into a past client at the Church meetings, Matthew Shelley. Perhaps he doesn't recognise her at first. The chances are that she would not recognise him. She would have had far too many punters to pick one out. Then it comes back to him who she was and that he had paid to have sex with her."

"He starts to spread rumours about her, talk to the congregation and the Vicar. Her fiancé, John Draper thinks Shelley is just a narrow minded bigot, but in fact he is sounding the water to see if Christine remembers him," said Mandy.

"He certainly had motive," said Sam.

"We are looking at the bigger picture remember. Shelley is not the only person who finds Christine's resurrection as Kelly unpalatable. Her pimp, Bobby Vasilescu, who came back from the States with her, was losing a good earner. Remember, they more or less set up the escort business in Eastbourne together. She is breaking away, setting up her own enterprise, taking clients away and probably some of the girls to boot. That would certainly put his nose out of joint."

"Would he kill her though?"

"Well I am guessing he would not lose sleep over giving the girls a good beating to get them in line," said Mandy.

"To be honest, my money was on Jeffery Abbot. We have him on CCTV at the station the night of the murder. He was obsessed with her, threatening her, stalking and his flat was plastered with photos taken while he followed her around," said Sam.

"Except it seems he came to Eastbourne, never went back to Brighton and yet he was back at his flat where someone murdered him there."

"It makes no sense."

"Well given the fact that he did not have a teleportation device, there is only one solution isn't there," said Mandy.

Sam looked puzzled. "There is?"

Mandy said nothing and passed Abbot's autopsy report to him. "He was murdered in his flat," said Sam.

"And there was an attempt to make it look like suicide. It tells us that someone was pretty keen to make it look like he had killed Christine. And ..."

"And...?" said Sam.

"Don't you see? It means that someone went through a hell of a lot of effort to make it look like Abbot was the killer. The knife, the blood stained hoody, his suicide and the CCTV all point to him. It all fitted."

"Except the autopsy," said Sam.

"Look at the report," continued Mandy. "Everything fits with suicide. The ligature marks are consistent with hanging himself but we struck lucky with the doctor that examined the body. There was only a slight mark on the neck that didn't match the ligature that he supposedly used by attaching it to the back of the door to hang himself."

Sam read for a moment. "I see. He was not strangled though. He was hung."

"Yes, but not by himself, in the process his killer pressed his thumb onto his neck causing a sub-dermal bruise that became apparent after death. He struggled to get Abbot's neck through the noose and used one hand to hoist his head up by the neck leaving the bruise."

"It could be his own thumb print as he tied he ligature," said Sam,

"No it couldn't. Let me show you." She stood up and placed her right hand round Sam throat. "See the bruise would be on the front left of you neck made with my fingers at the back of your neck. Now try and replicate that yourself."

Sam tried, He could just about get his thumb in the right spot but the was no possible way that he could get the fingers of his right hand to the back of his neck, "I see," he said. "So what do you think happened?"

"I think who ever killed him was in the flat with him. He, it has to be a man, because to hoist him up and hang him would take more strength than the average female would have. He either found Abbot semi-paralysed after taking Ketamine or more likely provided the drug. Either way, once the effects kicked in it was an easy matter to stage the suicide."

"That implies that Abbot knew the killer," said Sam.

"It also implies that the same person murdered Christine then travelled to Brighton and tried to fake the suicide of Abbot."

"We are looking for one killer," said Sam.

"I believe so, but there is a much more serious implication. It means that the evidence we gathered that demonstrates Abbot was Christine's killer needs to be looked at again, in the context that he was deliberately being framed as Christine's killer."

"You mean..."

"I mean everything, the knife, the stalking texts and emails, the hoody, the blood, everything," said Mandy.

Chapter 30

There was a knock on Mandy's door and Potts entered, "We bring tidings," waiting, behind him to see her and Sam, was Siskin.

"Wow," he continued, "You have one of those amazing sandwiches. They are brilliant aren't they? I don't know where they come up with their flavour combinations but they are just off the chart!"

Mandy looked at the remains of the half eaten sandwich that sat on her desk and thought she knew exactly where the manufacturers got their flavour combinations from, the compost heap at the local garden centre. She said nothing and smiled, offering the untouched half that remained in its wrapping to him.

"Thank you," he said but Mandy felt that his gratitude might well be short lived when he actually tasted it.

"Let's move outside as there seems to be a queue forming to see us." Moments later they were settled in the main area.

"Shoot," said Mandy to Siskin. "You best go first as DC Potts seems now be stuffing his face." Much to her surprise Potts gave her thumbs up." You can't account for taste," she thought as she watched him take a further bite.

"DNA results are in on Abbot's flat. As we thought, nothing on the knife we found. The hoody is a different matter. It is a smorgasbord of trace and DNA. Obviously Abbot's, the victim's was found on it. Christine Marstone's blood was found on it and the blood of an as yet unidentified other person."

"So what does that tell us?" said Mandy.

"It tells us that this was most likely the hoody we saw on CCTV in Eastbourne and that it came into contact with Christine. Her blood got on it when she was murdered in the Church car park," said Siskin.

"But more, it tells us that among the other bits of DNA on it, is the actual murderer's DNA. Abbot did not wear the hoody to Eastbourne that night. He never left his flat where he was later strangled. So we are being reasonable in supposing the person wearing the hoody was the person who killed Christine."

"So what are we saying?"

"I am saying that. The murderer made sure he was picked up in Eastbourne wearing the distinctive hoody, killed Christine then somehow left Eastbourne and went to meet with Abbot. He then possibly supplied Ketamine to Abbot and waited for him to become immobile. Somehow he persuaded Abbot to take a sufficient dose to put him in a virtual comatose state. Not that hard to do if he administered the dose or gave it to him without his knowledge. He put the hoody on his victim and killed him."

"In any event," Mandy continued. "The killers DNA has to be on that hoody."

"I ran all the samples through the database," interrupted

Constantinou. "No match, whoever it was, has no previous."

"Well, when we have a suspect we can test against the samples collected from the hoody and the victim," said Sam.

"We know quite a lot about the killer now. He was obviously connected closely to Christine. He had to know her whereabouts. He had to know of the fact that she was being stalked by Abbot. He had to know Abbot. We know from the CCTV that he was roughly the same build as Abbot and in his late thirties to early forties," said Merryweather.

"So we have an idea of the killers look, his movements and his physical appearance. We are getting closer. Anything else?" she said.

"The watch," said Merryweather. "We have a hit. It was stolen."

"Do we have details?" said Mandy.

"It looks like it was from a burglary in Chelsea. I am waiting on more information from the Met. It was on the usual stolen items list. I have sent them the number on all Rolex watches that makes it unique."

"One point, there was DNA on the inside of the metal strap of the watch. Abbots obviously, as it was on his wrist, but skin cells that were a match to some blood other than Christine's on the hoody."

"Merryweather, get onto the Met now and speak to the Detective in charge. Find out the details," said Mandy.

"Are you thinking what I am?" said Sam.

"That the hoody wearer wore the watch during and after he committed the burglary in Chelsea," said Mandy.

Before Sam could reply, Merryweather rejoined the group talking on the phone. "Just a moment, I need to put this on speaker," he said.

"I am Detective superintendent Parks," said the voice.

"DI Pile," said Mandy.

"We are investigating the murder of Raymond Stein at his house in Chelsea two months ago. The Rolex was the only thing taken from the scene."

Chapter 31

Detective superintendent Parks and DI Ellis, of the Metropolitan Serious Crime Unit were waiting in Mandy's office. It was eight o'clock that evening. They had driven to Eastbourne following the conversation earlier that day. Sam was keeping them company awaiting her arrival.

"I am so sorry to keep you waiting. I needed to go back to Brighton and got caught up in an accident just outside the town," she apologised breathlessly.

They rose as she entered and exchanged introductions. "It was clear when we drove down," said Ellis. Parks gave his DI a cautioning look. Ellis was right and there was no problem with traffic from Brighton to Eastbourne. Mandy had become delayed through her Mother's need to catch up on the latest news. She had been waiting for Mandy when she had returned to her flat to change.

"I can only apologise again," said Mandy as she took her seat. Sam had retrieved the Rolex watch from the evidence and it sat before them on the desk.

Parks spoke and glossed over the subject. "No problem, we are grateful for the cooperation. We have had a look at the watch and there is no doubt it belongs to our murder victim Raymond Stein. So the question is how did your murder victim, Jeffrey Abbot come to be in possession of it?"

"I am not altogether sure if we can answer that. I will give you the brief background to our case. Mandy went on to explain that they were investigating the murder of Christine Marstone and that their inquiries had led them to Abbot as their prime suspect.

"So you first thoughts were that this chap Abbot has been stalking your victim, killed her and then in remorse killed himself?"

"Yes, but it seems he was murdered and did not commit suicide. In any event, the time line doesn't work." She went on to explain that it was clear someone dressed in a hoody, killed Christine, planted it on Abbot and then strangled him.

"That does not prevent Abbot knifing our victim Raymond Stein and stealing the Rolex," said Parks.

"I suppose not, but have you any connection between Abbot and Stein?" said Sam.

"Nothing, but we do have CCTV of the murderer from the camera that records visitors to Stein's gaff," said Ellis.

"Let's see it then," said Mandy.

Moments later they watched as the footage was played on Ellis's tablet. The camera was positioned to capture anyone on the doorstep to Stein's. A figure wearing a hoody could be seen pressing the door bell. The door opened and he went inside. Seven minutes later the same figure was captured leaving.

"You can't make out the face," observed Mandy.

"No, it is clear that the murderer was aware of the camera and kept the hood up and his face away from the camera," said Ellis.

Sam pushed the hoody across the desk in a clear plastic evidence bag. Parks picked it up and gave it a close inspection, "Looks identical to the one on the CCTV."

"There is little doubt. We have recovered multiple samples of DNA and now forensics know what to look for, I am pretty confident that we will get a match to your victim. We will push to get the analysis done," said Mandy.

"That still leaves us with the problem of who was wearing it?"

"We can also assume that the killers DNA is among the multitude of other samples on it," said Sam.

"And you haven't got a hit on any?" said Ellis.

"No, if someone is framing Abbot they are not in the system," said Sam.

"As it stands it looks like our prime suspect has to be Jeffrey Abbot. The hoody was found in his possession and his physical appearance matches the caller the night Stein was murdered. As Stein admitted his killer he must have known him," said Parks.

"So if we run with that, then we end up with a situation whereby Abbot, having killed Stein is then framed for the murder of Christine Marstone and is then murdered himself. The killer in the intervening period comes into the possession of Abbot's hoody, which he wears to kill Christine.

"That all seems a bit far-fetched though. Don't you feel," said Ellis.

"Well, my thinking is that we are assuming that Abbot is working alone. The facts could easily support two killers working together. Look at it this way. Someone wants Stein and Marstone dead. Abbot and the unknown second perpetrator kill Stein. There is some form disagreement over payment..."said Mandy

"Or the fact that Abbot takes the watch that he may be planning to sell. He was a drug user and may have become a liability. His accomplice sees the opportunity to kill two birds with one stone, get rid of Abbot who has become a liability and use his fixation on Christine to pin her murder on him, leaving himself in the clear," said Sam

"It was only the astuteness of the forensics that spotted the bruise on Abbots neck that confirmed he was murdered, otherwise we would have accepted the scenario that Abbot killed Christine and then committed suicide. Her DNA on the hoody and the knife would have removed the need to investigate further, case closed," said Mandy.

"We need to establish what the connection is between Abbot and Stein," said Ellis. "Was he and an associate hired to kill him and if so who and why?"

"I don't buy it. It is too much of a coincidence. It means that Christine was murdered for no other motive than to set Abbot up," said Mandy.

"Stein was a very wealthy individual, worth billions. You don't make that sort of money without making lots of enemies. We have a list as long as your arm of people who had a grievance against him, businessmen who lost everything to him for example," said Ellis.

"What about people who directly benefited from his death. Who got money?" said Mandy.

"Most of it went to charity. He had already settled vast sums directly and indirectly on his only real companions, Vera Reynolds his personal assistant and Timothy Welling his driver. They had no reason to want him dead."

"Wife, kids..?"

"No children and his wife was killed in a car crash years ago."

"Well somebody wanted him dead and he knew whoever it was because he opened his door and let them in," said Mandy.

Well our best suspect is Jeffery Abbot, a junkie that killed him and stole his watch worth a couple of hundred thousand quid," said Ellis.

"To be fair, what happened to Abbot and if he committed suicide or got himself murdered is not our investigation but yours. If we get a match of Stein's DNA to the hoody Abbot was wearing then we have our killer," said Parks.

Chapter 32

"Well they were a fat lot of help," said Mandy as Parks and Ellis left to go back to London.

"I know, but they are struggling with a shortage of man power like the rest of us and they have a lot more murders to deal with than we do," said Sam.

"It's just like everyone wants the case closed as quickly as possible."

"Well at least Parks has made their files available to us. I will get the team to go over them and see if they can tie anything back to our murders," said Sam.

Mandy slumped back into her chair as Sam left to divide up the Met's files among the team. He had a list of references and pass codes supplied by Ellis. These would allow them access, via their Police Computer terminals, to the data stored online.

She knew she was not seeing the whole picture. There were suspects and motives. She ran through the list of names in her mind.

John Draper, the fiancée with strict religious parents and

himself a Christian, finding out his future wife was a call girl was reason enough to want her gone. They had found her phone hidden at his house. It contained the contact details of her clients. Had she hidden it or had he. Had he found it and discovered who he was actually marrying. They had established he could have followed her to the car park and stabbed her. He had blood on him, supposedly when he cradled her in his arms on finding her.

Matthew Shelley was fearful of being identified by Christine. Had she perhaps been blackmailing him? She thought not, but again he had the opportunity and he had been overheard attacking her verbally to the Reverend Grant.

The Reverend Grant, fearful of his proclivity for children being discovered could not totally be discounted. Mandy was sure that he had killed himself knowing that it was only a matter of time before the police discovered the child pornography on his laptop. Did Christine in her line of work somehow suspect or have evidence of his paedophilia? Mandy doubted it.

What about her pimp, Bobby Vasilescu? They had a long and profitable association going back to when they met in the USA. Was he angry at her leaving his stable of escorts and setting up her own business? She was running gangbang parties along the south coast, Hastings, Eastbourne and Brighton as well as other locations. She had enticed some of the girls to work with her, Kelly Albright for one.

Jeffery Abbot was clearly the key to the whole affair but how? The night of Christine's murder he had not left Brighton, or to be accurate, his phone hadn't. He was fixated with the victim and was rebuffed by her. He fitted the stalker pattern that so many times saw young women attacked and murdered. There was no doubt that in his mind he had a relationship with her. She, on the other hand, saw only a delusional ex-client. There was no clear evidence that he was not at

Eastbourne railway station wearing the hoody. If it were Abbot, then he must have had some means of getting back to Brighton other than by bus, train or taxi. He did not have a car nor had he hired one. It seemed highly unlikely that he had hitchhiked.

She rubbed her eyes and tried to sort the facts in her mind. The hoody was the key. It had been present at the murder of Raymond Steins, the murder of Christine Marstone and was found at the scene of Jeffery Abbot's murder. It was awash with DNA of all the victims and probably the killers as well, as probably, a whole host of unconnected people it had been in contact with.

She struggled to see any connection with the murder of Stein, a retired billionaire businessman and Abbot or Christine. The only connection was the hoody and a stolen watch found on Abbot. The watch clearly linked Abbot to Stein and a possible robbery motive.

Questions formed in Mandy's mind as she reviewed the facts in the case so far. One, why would Stein open the door to his killer? A hooded figure, avoiding his face being caught on the CCTV is apparently just let it. Stein, according to the reports, was more or less a reclusive after the death of his wife.

She tapped a few keys and looked up the details gathered by Parks and Ellis on her laptop. She was surprised to see that he was planning to remarry. The saying 'old fool and money soon parted.' sprang into her head. She soon realised, reading on, that ever the businessman he had approached the whole matter in a truly dispassionate matter and instructed a leading law firm to draw up the contract between them and adapting his will to reflect it. It was more or less a business relationship. She would give him company and she would have a generous allowance and fifty million on his death. Mandy saw that all the paper work had been completed.

The girl's name was Tracy Bright. On reading further she saw that neither Stein's housekeeper. Vera Reynolds, nor his chauffeur Tim Welling, had seen her for two months prior to his murder. Mandy, as had Parks, realised she had a massive motive for wanting Stein dead. The obvious conclusion to be drawn was that she had hired Abbot and perhaps another to murder Stein.

She read on looking for more background on Tracy Bright. The Met had a massive effort to locate her. They had no success to date. It seemed as if she had disappeared from the face of the Earth. They only had her name to go on. They had no DNA, no history and they could not even be sure of her nationality. It was clearly an enormous tasks to find her if she did not want to be found.

She got up and headed to the coffee machine. She walked through the office and noted with satisfaction that her team were all hard at work. She took the cup from the machine and shuddered at the taste from her first sip. She made her way back and decided to make a progress round around her team and offer words of encouragement.

Merryweather was dealing with the scene of crime forensic report at Stein's Murder. Passing, Mandy glimpsed the interior of Stein's house on his laptop. "Wow that's what I call a house and a half," she said.

"It's a flipping palace, look at the size of it." He scrolled the photos across the screen. Room after room, all massive in size, beautifully decorated, designed and opulently furnished. Scrolling across he joked. "Can I have a pay rise?"

Mandy had to admit that despite her own privileged upbringing this was a totally different level of wealth. She knew that a house like this was in itself worth in excess of thirty million. Most of Stein's wealth was to go to a charitable foundation, which he had already endowed with over one hundred million during his lifetime. That was set to increase ten-fold on his death. She realised from his point of view his dalliance with Tracy was no more than pocket change.

She had to admit that his London house was jaw dropping. "If you think that is something, you should she his house and yacht in Florida. He has the US President as a neighbour," said Merryweather.

"Is it relevant to the murder?" she asked faking disapproval.

"Well, no not really but it is unbelievable."

"Curiosity for how the mega rich lived got the better of her. "Go on then, let's have a look."

The shots of the house, now up for sale were stunning. There was even a video tour. Merryweather pressed play. The camera went from stunning room to stunning room. There were works of art, everywhere, paintings and sculpture dotted around. They were both fascinated at the spectacle.

. "Stop," said Mandy suddenly. "Go back."

Merryweather went back, "what are you looking at?" he asked.

"That," she pointed to the screen.

"Oh my God," Merryweather sounded shocked.

There staring out to them from the laptop was a photo of Raymond Stein with his arm around a young bikini clad woman, clearly taken on a yacht. "That's Christine Marstone," she said.

Chapter 33

"The man's a bloody idiot," said Sam. He had just come off the phone to DI Ellis.

"What did he say," asked Mandy?

"He said they did look for Tracy Bright and it is ongoing. They don't even have a photograph of her and they have no DNA so there was no hit on our murder victim when we did a database search."

"But they said Stein was to marry her and she was left millions on his death. How was his lawyer to identify her and give her the money? His lawyer must have details surely?" she said.

"Well they are not completely stupid, they contacted the firm of solicitors who are administering the estate. It was a dead end from the police's point of view. The money is in trust in a bank account waiting for her to claim it."

"How is she to do that?"

"She has to go to the solicitor's who will access the account. She has to key in her date of birth, real name and the solicitor has to enter a code and the money will be transferred to the account she designates. Stein probably told her all this before his death."

"All a bit cloak and dagger isn't it?"

"Parks and Ellis asked the solicitor why the complexity. It seems that Stein was certainly aware of Christine come Tracy's colourful past. The solicitor did not get the full story from him, but there were two reasons for the way it was to be done. Firstly, it was clear that Stein was no fool and he knew full well that this was more of a business transaction than a love match. Effectively, the money was held in escrow until she completed on the marriage. Secondly, it was, according to the solicitor, a matter of confidentiality. He got the impression that she was breaking from a chequered past and that they may have been some personal risk to her."

"In other words he feared who might crawl out the woodwork if it was known that Christine, AKA Tracy and AKA Kelly was going to be worth millions. He had a point. That sleaze ball Vasilescu for one would certainly be in the gunning to try and get a slice of the cake," said Mandy.

"What happened on Stein's death? Does she still get the money?" said Sam.

"I assume it depends on who dies first. If she died before him then obviously her estate does not benefit. If he dies first then the Will is executed and she inherits."

"But they never married?" said Sam.

"From what you say it was a trust fund that became hers on marriage or on Stein's death."

"So she gets the money because she was murdered after Stein was murdered?"

"And it would pass to her next of kin or if she made a Will the beneficiary under the terms of her it. To access it they would need to turn up with her death certificate at the lawyer's office and know her real name," said Mandy.

"Her father would be her next of kin as no Will of hers has turned up," said Sam.

"The question is: did he know about Stein and Christine?"

In a bid to answer that question, Mandy and Sam pulled up outside the block of flats in Edmonton some three hours later. "Let's hope the car still has wheels on it when we get back," said Sam as he locked the car and followed Mandy to Marstone's flat.

They knocked on the door for over ten minutes. The neighbour, hearing the noise, confirmed that he was indeed at home. Eventually they received a response, "Who is it?" Mr Marstone was clearly slurring his speech.

"Great, he's pissed," said Sam.

"It's the police, Mr Marstone. Can we have a word?" said Mandy.

The door opened a little and his face appeared. "What the fuck do you want now?"

"There's no need for that language now is there Sir," said Sam.

"Fuck off," he replied.

Mandy realised that Mr Marstone was clearly not the friendliest of drunks. She also realised that they did not want to waste time and effort getting involved in nicking Christine's father for a public order offence. "You remember me, don't you? I am trying to catch your daughter's killer, Christine?"

"My Christine, my Christine, my poor Christine," he began to lament.

Sam rolled his eyes. He found it hard to disguise his contempt for this man. He had done precious little for his daughter as a child and now he was all bleeding hearts now she was dead. Mandy gave Sam a stern look. He kept his feelings to himself.

"Yes your Christine," she coaxed.

"Have you found the bastard that murdered her?"

"No, not yet but we need you help?"

"What?"

"Did you know she was getting married?" said Sam.

Marstone opened the door wider and stood swaying slightly as he took in what Sam had said, "Getting married?"

"She was about to marry?"

"Getting married," he repeated, "To who?"

"Did you know?" Mandy said, but it was clear that he had no clue as to her liaison with Raymond Stein.

"She's married?" he said.

"No," said Sam.

"I don't understand," Marstone was rambling in his speech.

Mandy realised that there was little more to be gained by talking to him and made her goodbyes. She and Sam returned to the car.

"That was a waste of time," said Sam.

"I think we can safely assume that her father had no idea about her arrangement with Stein. Even if he did, there is no way he killed him and his daughter to get his hands on the money."

"That's pretty obvious given his state. You're right. We can safely knock him off our list of suspects.

"Okay, just one last visit and then back to sunny Eastbourne," she said.

They had called ahead and Vera Reynolds was expecting them. She was a pleasant contrast to their meeting with the drunk and belligerent Marstone. "Coffee, tea?" she asked as they settled in the lounge. Both Sam and Mandy accepted the offer. It was clear that Vera was not your average secretary. The fact that she had a butler who served the tea was a clear indication of that.

Mandy spoke first. "Would you look at this photograph, "she said passing a picture of the deceased Christine Marstone to her.

"That's Tracy, Mr Stein's fiancée," she said without hesitation.

"And this picture?" she handed a printout of the photo in the frame they had spotted in Stein's Florida mansion. It showed Stein and Christine, in a bathing costume aboard a yacht.

"Oh my God, I had forgotten all about that picture. Detective Parks asked me if there were any photos of Tracy and I said no. It just completely went out of my mind. I need to contact him."

"No need, we have dealt with that. More to the point, was the picture taken in Miami?" Mandy knew that Christine had been deported from America and yet it appeared as if she had somehow returned with Stein avoiding US Immigration.

Vera laughed. "It looks like given the blue sea and sky. No, It was taken on a friend of Raymond's boat, at Cowes in the Solent. We went to the Isle of Wight for a few days."

That cleared up part of the mystery. "How did it get to Mr Stein's house in Florida?"

"He had decided to sell the estate there. He asked Tracy to go with him for a holiday. She could not go for some reason. I don't recall why, so he went on his own. He hired a private jet and met with the agent from Sotheby's out there. He was gone about five days in all. I assume he took the photo with him and must have left it."

Sitting in the traffic on the drive back to Eastbourne, Mandy had plenty of time to mull over the murder of Christine Marstone. As they sat in the queue of traffic on the M23 heading past Gatwick Airport watching the planes overhead, she began to see clearly.

"I know who committed the murder," she said.

Chapter 34

It was past ten when they arrived back at the Station. Sam was still pondering Mandy's statement. As they pulled up he said. "You know who killed Christine?"

"There is only one logical solution but I still need one piece of evidence to confirm my theory."

"Well?"

"I need to wait for a reply to something to be certain," she said. "In the meantime we need to reconstruct the events the night Christine was murdered. Arrange for all the key players to be at the Church tomorrow at the same time. Now I am going home to bed.

The next day Mandy arrived late. The team were already out collecting the participants to the reconstruction when she arrived at the Station. Sam looked at her and waited for her to enlighten him. "Did you get what you wanted?" he asked.

She patted an envelope on her desk. "All will be revealed," she smiled.

They left the station and made their way to the Church Hall.

Meryweather had collected John Draper, Siskin had Matthew Shelley and Potts had Bobby Vasilescu in tow. Constantinou had a video camera to record events. It was beginning to get dark as they stopped in the car park.

They made their way inside and pulled up chairs to form a circle. "Good evening, thank you for coming," she said.

"We weren't given much choice," said Shelley.

"I am sure all of you would want to help find the killer of a young woman, so a little inconvenience is a small price to pay. I am sure you will agree?" she continued. "The main thing is that we are all here."

Sam spoke, "we are going to run through that nights events as they occurred. DC Constantinou will act as Christine and I shall be the Reverend Grant, as they cannot obviously be present."

"Let's start with you Mr Shelley talking to the Reverend Grant. Where were you exactly?" Matthew Shelley took up his position and Sam acting as the Vicar joined him.

"Now where were you Mr Draper and where was Christine?" Mandy continued. He made his way past Sam and Shelley, positioning Constantinou already in the Hall as Christine."

"What happened next?"

"Draper answered, "after the lesson we started the silent contemplation."

"Who left first?"

"It was the Vicar," said Shelley. Draper nodded his agreement.

"Then Christine?"

"No, I think it was me," said Draper.

"And I joined the Vicar," said Shelley.

Mandy looked at Sam. "It is clear now seeing the layout that anyone of you had the opportunity to follow Christine out, kill her and you all had a motive."

"Let's begin with you Mr Draper. You were her fiancé but you did not really know her. You met her and fell in love, but you only knew her as Kelly Albright. Did you discover from her phone, email or perhaps a third party what she really was, a common prostitute?"

He started to protest his love for her. Mandy ignored him and continued. "Did you feel betrayed, enraged and a fool? How would your highly pious parents react on discovering their son was marrying a whore? You wanted out and killing her would solve all the embarrassment."

She silenced his denials and turned her attention to Matthew Shelley. "Of course you too feared exposure. You had used Christine's services. Your whole World was at risk, you a pillar of the Community, a Christian and as it turns out, a possible future Conservative Party candidate for parliament. I did some checks earlier today and the Chairman of the local Association confirms that you had political ambitions," said Mandy.

"I wouldn't kill anyone," he said.

"Not even to protect your reputation, perhaps not?" she said.

"Now we need to look at Jeffrey Abbot," she said. "He was infatuated with our victim. He was delusional and in his mind saw her as his love. He was addicted to drugs and highly unstable. He had a hoody with her blood on it. He could have travelled here and waited for her, incensed at being spurned and furious, he killed her as she stepped out to the car park for a cigarette. He of course cannot answer as he is now dead."

"Why am I here? I was not even at the Church the night she was murdered," interrupted Bobby Vasilescu.

"But you could have been and you had a motive did you not? She was one of your girls. Girls you made money from introducing them to men for sex. She wasn't playing ball and had started to work on her own account. You couldn't let that happen. You had to send a message to the other girls so they didn't get the same idea."

There was an expectant silence in the hall as they resumed their seats. "I will tell you a series of events that led to the murder of Christine Marstone and who committed it. Please do not attempt to leave. My officers have orders to detain anyone who does."

Chapter 35

"We need to go back a few years and to another continent," began Mandy.

"Christine Marstone is in Las Vegas, down on her luck, getting by working as a waitress and sometime common prostitute. Things are tough, but things improve when she meets Bobby Vasilescu. He is surviving on the margins, hustling, thieving and a bit of drug dealing. At some point they become lovers."

"Christine, now has a protector, a pimp in Bobby. Life becomes easier for her to ply her trade. He ensured her safety as well as dealing weed. Life is a little easier and they get by. They are still interlopers and taking business from the local pimps and their girls. It could not last and it doesn't. They are brought to the attention of the police and Christine is arrested and having outstayed her visa is returned to the UK. He follows her back, either out of genuine love for her or purely for financial reasons. It is hard to say."

"Virtually penniless, she has to continue her activities as a prostitute. At some stage they rent an office on an industrial estate in Eastbourne and set up the escort service. Gradually, Bobby encourages more girls to sign up and they are making a living. Although located in Eastbourne, where the rent and rates are cheaper, they cater mainly to the London market. The business consists of little more than a web site and a phone answering service that operates twenty four seven. The punter phones the agency, select a girl and the agency texts or phones the girls the address. For each booking they get, Bobby and Christine take a cut."

"At some stage Raymond Stein books Christine and for whatever reason, he takes to her and a relationship of sorts begins. At first he knows her as Tracy, her working name. She becomes almost his regular companion. His driver would pick her up and drop her off. He is a generous man and Bobby Vasilescu is more than pleased with the arrangement."

"Things start to unravel with her and Bobby. She has become tired of prostituting herself and handing her money to him. She decides enough is enough and branches out on her own. She starts running sex parties with some of the girls she has met. They find a location, usually a private house and Christine and two or three girls would turn up and gangbang upwards of sixteen or twenty men. They run two parties, one at lunch time and one in the evening. The men pay around a hundred pounds each to gangbang the girls."

"Matthew Shelley attended on one such party. He became more involved and In return for providing the venue, he got to attend and participate in the two sex parties for free." Mandy glanced across to see the man squirming uncomfortably in his seat.

"I am not clear when Christine first met John Draper," she continued. "I assume it was during the break between the afternoon and evening gangbang at Shelley's flat," she did not wait for Draper to respond. "In any event they become acquainted and matters progress between them. Christine gives him the name Kelly Albright on their first meeting. It is a normal precaution in her line of work to not give out your real name. She could not have known that the relationship would progress with Draper at that stage. When they fell in love, she was trapped in the lie."

"You, Mr Vasilescu, became aware that not only had Christine deserted your stable of girls, but had actually set up a rival business and she was even running sex parties in Eastbourne, right on your doorstep. You were angry at this."

"In your statement Mr Draper, you said on evening you met with Christine and by this stage you were lovers and she stayed over at your flat once or twice a month. On this occasion, when you met, she was bloodied and bruised. She claimed to have been mugged and you took her to the District hospital."

"That's right," he confirmed.

"In fact that was untrue wasn't it, Mr Vasilescu?" said Mandy directing her gaze at him. He remained silent. "In fact Mr Vasilescu, you tracked her down and gave her a beating to warn her off. Is that not the case?"

There was no response. Mandy continued. "She checked herself out of the hospital the following day and decided to avoid Eastbourne and Vasilescu. She put her relationship with Draper on hold."

"Christine, in a bid to avoid matters, moves in with the actual Kelly Albright in London. All the while Raymond Stein is pushing on with his plan tp marry her. She at some stage tells him her real name but also reveals that she is in fear of further violence from Bobby Vasilescu. It must be assumed that Stein is probably fully aware of Vasilescu, as it was he that arranged the liaisons with Christine through his escort agency. Stein, along with his solicitor constructed a slightly convoluted method to ensure that Christine's identity remained protected, whilst ensuring she would benefit from the trust fund and pre-nuptial agreement. Put simply, she would receive fifty million to marry him."

"Of course Christine has met John Draper and does no longer

want to marry Stein after all. But there is the matter of the fifty million to consider. I cannot be sure when she decided she does not want to continue with the arrangement but that is what happens."

"She is living with Kelly Albright, seemingly out of reach of her past life and especially Vasilescu. Things are not ideal as Kelly has her problems with drugs but Christine feels relatively safe."

"But things take a dramatic turn. Out of nowhere you, Bobby Vasilescu, turn up. Somehow you have become aware of Raymond Stein's plan to marry Christine. I am guessing he contacted you in an attempt to locate his missing bride to be. He probably discloses the fact they were to marry and that she was to get a vast amount of money as part of the deal."

Mandy again spoke directly to Vasilescu. "Is that what happened. Did Stein tell you about the money?"

Vasilescu returned her gaze defiantly and said nothing.

"No matter," said Mandy and continued the narrative.

"You attempt to force Christine to go back and reunite with Stein. You demand that she shares the money with you. I am unsure as to the exact sequence of events that follow. Christine moves in with Kelly Albright but she ends up in hospital following a drugs overdose."

"Kelly's parents appear at the hospital. In all probability Christine contacted them on Kelly's behalf. Events take a turn in Christine's favour when Kelly's mother and father invite her to travel and stay with them in Bristol. Christine seizes the opportunity and the chance of a new start away from, Vasilescu, Stein and her life as a prostitute."

"Tragedy strikes. After stopping at the service area, the car they are travelling in is struck by a lorry as they re-join the M4 motorway. Kelly and her parents are killed in the crash. Confused and dazed but alive, Christine makes a fateful decision. She takes the identity of her friend. Unobserved she leaves the scene of the accident and makes her way back to the service area on foot."

"She now has a new identity as Kelly Albright. She needs to get away from the scene of the crash. There is only one person that knows her as Kelly and that is John Draper. She calls him and he drives from Eastbourne and collects her."

"She is now clear of her past and ready to start a new life with the man she loves."

Chapter 36

"So who killed Christine and why," said Mandy. "To find the answer we need to go back in time a little. But first I think we need to look at how the murder was accomplished."

"There is one person that I have left out of the picture so far and that is Jeffery Abbot. Abbot was a loner that lived in Brighton. Through the Escort Agency he became acquainted with Christine. He was a habitual drug user and Ketamine was he preferred choice. He was also a fantasist. In his mind he created and convinced himself that he and Christine were lovers, that she was his girlfriend. He was fixated with her and became her stalker. He would send her emails discussing their future life together."

"Of course, this was not reciprocated by Christine and after initially trying to placate and humour him, she became increasingly aggressive in her rejection of him and the nuisance he was."

She addressed Vasilescu. "I assume it was your job to deal with such problems as Abbot when your girls encountered them? Did you have reason to have words with him?"

Vasilescu sat impassively. "I won't be drawn into anything," he said

"Okay, that is your right," said Mandy. "I, on the other hand have no such constraints. So here is how I think it went."

"You made contact with Abbot, initially to warn him off. You are not particularly successful as he continues to harass her even after she no longer works for you. You realise in any event he is more a nuisance than a threat, so refrain from the use of violence, perhaps you even try and get him to use the services of another one of the girls. After all he is a paying customer."

"We need to go back in time to understand the murder of Christine Marstone, to the night of the death of Raymond Stein. Picture the scene. Stein is home alone, his house keeper and driver have departed. There is a ring on the doorbell. He checks the camera that is positioned covering the porch. He sees a figure, face turned away, wearing a distinctive hood, yet he still lets him in."

"It is the last thing he does. He is killed within moments and one item, one item only is taken, the watch, a very unique and easily identifiable watch, a Rolex. Nothing else is disturbed or stolen and the killer leaves."

"Then weeks later we see the same very distinctive hoody leave Eastbourne Railway Station. Our murderer then finds Christine here in the car park and kills her." Mandy paused and studied the faces for any sign of reaction.

"The hooded figure then effectively vanishes. There is no sign of him leaving Eastbourne and returning to Brighton where Jeffrey Abbot lives and yet the hoody and the Rolex watch appear back in Abbot's flat, where we find him having apparently killed himself in a fit of remorse after killing Christine. It is impossible, unless Abbot has some sort of teleportation device available to him."

"This is what actually happened. Our killer, yes there is only the one, at some stage takes Abbot's hoody from his flat. He is careful to minimise the amount of his DNA on it. He goes to Wickes, the building supply store in Eastbourne and purchases a pack of coverall white painting suits. They are more or less what the forensics team wear when they attend a crime scene."

"How do we know this? Firstly, on closer study of the CCTV at Stein's and Eastbourne Station, we can get a glimpse of the white of the suit peeking from under the hoody. Then it was just a matter of trolling Wickes till receipts and in store CCTV footage. No real proof other than one of you here decided to do a bit of decorating."

"He enters the station in Eastbourne with the white overall and the hoody in a plastic bag. He goes to the toilets where he puts them on. He waits for the arrival of the train from Brighton and joins the passengers exiting, making sure he is caught on camera but ensures his face is turned away."

"He goes to the Church, kills Christine and removes the hoody and overalls. He retains the hoody and dumps the white suit. He then gets in his car and drives to Brighton. An hour later he kills Abbot and leaves the hoody and the Rolex watch."

"It was perfect except the autopsy detected the bruise from the killer's thumb, that meant that Abbot had not committed suicide. As all but one of you were at the Church, you could not have been at the Station dressed in Abbots hoody. All of you, that is except you Mr Vasilescu."

"Mr Vasilescu I am arresting you for the murder of Raymond Stein, Jeffrey Abbot and Christine Marstone. You do not need to say anything but anything you do say may be…."

Chapter 37

Sam was looking doubtful as Vasilescu was led away. "Can we prove it?"

Mandy handed him a piece of paper. "I obtained this from the police in Nevada. It was what I was waiting on."

"It's a marriage certificate between Bobby Vasilescu and Christine Marstone."

"It is indeed. They were married in the USA. When she was deported and returned to the UK, they set up the escort service. Vasilescu's wife was the first prostitute in its employ."

"He knew all about Stein's offer of marriage and the vast amount of money involved. They worked together to get his money in escrow. They were unconcerned about the marriage in the States. It would never be picked up over here."

"So what happened?"

"For some reason she changed her mind. Perhaps she had enough of Bobby. Maybe she saw him for the free loading scum bag he was or she might even have developed a conscience about deceiving

Stein. We may never know, but we do not that she was not willing to see it through."

"And Vasilescu killed her in anger?" said Sam.

"No greed?"

"I don't understand?"

"When Stein died, she inherited the fifty million. When she died without making a will her next of kin inherited."

"Her father?"

"No her husband, Vasilescu," said Mandy. "When he couldn't get her to go through with the marriage to Stein he had to act. He cultivated Abbot, supplying him with drugs and keeping in contact with him. It was easy to take his hoody."

"Stein?"

"He knew that Stein was desperately looking for Christine. I assumed Stein knew that Vasilescu was her pimp at some stage. So the night of the murder he turns up and says that he has news of Christine's whereabouts. Stein lets him in. He kills him wearing, Abbots hoody and gets his blood on it."

"Now to get his hands on the money, he has only to kill Christine. She has no idea Stein is dead and she has inherited millions. The night of her murder, Vasilescu puts on the hoody at the railway station and heads for the Church where he murders his wife."

"So he is never on the train from Brighton and of course that is why we could not trace Abbot going back."

"Vasilescu gets in his car, which was always in Eastbourne and drive to Abbot's, kills him, stages the suicide, returns his hoody and plants the watch."

"Then all he has to do, is wait for the dust to settle and come forward with the marriage certificate and claim the money from Christine's estate. In the meantime Abbot takes the rap."

"Can we prove it," said Sam?

"We have identified Vasilescu's DNA on the Hoody, now we have taken a sample from him on his arrest. There was also a sample on the Rolex watch proving he took it from Stein. We have CCTV and ANPR identifying his car travelling to Brighton on the night of Abbots murder."

"The receipts for the purchase of the white suits he wore to the murders," added Sam.

"I am pretty sure that we will find CCTV of him travelling to London and leaving the underground station the night he murdered Stein. Now we know who we are looking for and given the number of CCTV cameras in the area where Stein lived, we will probably be able to track him all the way there and back. He will be placed at the scene both by forensics and by CCTV."

"An examination of his cell phone revealed that he was the one that placed a tracker on Christine's phone. He knew her every movement and was aware that she was in Eastbourne and living with Draper."

"Well, the Crown Prosecution Service are taking it forward on all three counts of murder. Well done," said Chief Super Intendent Taylor. "Not only did you solve Christine Marstone's murder, you solved Abbot's and the Mets' murder of Stein to boot, not to mention the murder of a child for the Sheffield police, exposed the Reverend Grant as a paedophile and the cover up by the Church."

"I think I am getting the hang of this Detective stuff, Sir."

Printed in Great
Britain
by Amazon